MW00937455

Cover Copy

There can be only one...for both of them.

In the twelfth century, a man named Gilleoin was gifted with the ability to shift into a bear. His clan was called Matheson, and when he mated with a woman carrying faerie blood, they created a line shrouded in secrecy, yet still, far into the future, whispers would abound...

For five long years, Isla Matheson has run from the one man her fae ancestor prophesized would be hers, but now her time for running is done. Her shifter mate is closing in and when he captures her and takes her home to his clan, she can no longer deny either of them. She chooses to merge with him in all ways, and in doing so sets a twelfth century prophecy in motion, one that sends her hurtling back through time to when their clan first began.

Highland warrior shifter Iain Matheson has fallen under his mate's spell. She's the one woman he would die to protect, and when a portal opens and takes her from him, he dives in after her. He'll never allow her to escape him, not even when he becomes embroiled in one of the greatest feuds raging at that time.

Now they have a mission, to save their future line from extinction, to give hope to their people, both in the future and the past.

Books by Joanne Wadsworth

The Matheson Brothers Series
Highlander's Desire, Book One
Highlander's Passion, Book Two
Highlander's Seduction, Book Three

Highlander Heat Series
Highlander's Castle, Book One
Highlander's Magic, Book Two
Highlander's Charm, Book Three
Highlander's Guardian, Book Four
Highlander's Faerie, Book Five
Highlander's Champion, Book Six
Highlander's Captive (Short Story)

Magio-Earth Series
Protector, Book One
Warrior, Book Two
Enchanter, Book Three
Hunter (Short Story)

Bodyguards Series
Witness Pursuit, Book One
Bodyguard Pursuit, Book Two

Highlander's Desire

The Matheson Brothers, Book One

by Joanne Wadsworth

Highlander's Desire
ISBN-13: 978-1-51233-782-2
ISBN-10: 1-51233-782-X
Copyright © 2015, Joanne Wadsworth
Cover Art by Joanne Wadsworth
First electronic publication: April 2015

Joanne Wadsworth
http://www.joannewadsworth.com

All Rights Are Reserved. No part of this book may be used or reproduced in any manner whatsoever without written permission, except in the case of brief quotations embodied in critical articles and reviews. The unauthorized reproduction or distribution of this copyrighted work is illegal. No part of this book may be scanned, uploaded or distributed via the Internet or any other means, electronic or print, without the author's permission.

AUTHOR'S NOTE:
This book is a work of fiction. The names, characters, places, and incidents are products of the writer's imagination or have been used fictitiously and are not to be construed as real. Any resemblance to persons, living or dead, actual events, locale or organizations is entirely coincidental. The author does not have any control over and does not assume any responsibility for third-party websites or their content.

Published in the United States of America

First digital publication: April 2015
First print publication: May 2015

Acknowledgements

I have an incredibly supportive family who allow me so much time to write. Huge thanks go to my hubby, Jason, and kiddies, Marisa, Caleb, Cruise and Rocco. Hugs.

For my readers, I can't thank you enough for joining me, and taking this journey to where imagination and magic soar.

The Prophecy

The ancient House of Clan Matheson, Scotland, 1190.

Sorcha screamed as pain gripped her belly and racked through her.

"Your twin bairns wish to be born, my dear." Nessa, Sorcha's mother and their clan's fae-blooded seer, knelt at her bedside. "I see a vision of them. Two lads of mayhap eight or nine. They're very strong."

"What else do ye see?" Panting, Sorcha fisted the bed sheet either side of her.

"They're tussling and giggling in a meadow as Gilleoin watches on." Nessa caught her hand. "Your sons are so very like their father. They can shift shape, call forth their inner bear, and draw claws."

"Are ye certain?" She longed to give her husband bairns who held his revered ability, one gifted to him by The Most High One. Gilleoin was the first and only known man to hold shifter blood. The night she'd first met him, five years past, had been when he'd sailed along the loch to her village, strode right toward her and gazing into her eyes, lowered to one knee. He'd declared, under the brilliance of the full moon, that a mated bond had formed between them and she was his. She'd sensed the bond too, to the depths of her soul, with her sudden need to touch him and the pure aura of energy surrounding him. Some of her village people, those directly descended from the faerie prince who'd wed their chief's daughter two centuries past, held a touch of fae blood and as such also held rare and divine skills. Upon her birth, she'd received the ability of aura reading and could perceive another's true intentions. Gilleoin's aura drew her toward him and later that night when she'd lain with him, he'd merged their minds with his shifter ability and forged a link along a pathway known only to them. His shifter blood was strong, and though he held not a touch of fae blood and wasn't one of her people, he was still hers and always would be so.

"Very certain, and there's more." Swaying, Mother closed her eyes, her red locks wisped with gray coiled high upon her head. "Your eldest son and his descendants shall possess the skills of our fae people, although your youngest son willnae. He and his progeny shall be shifter alone."

"What skill will my eldest be gifted with?"

"That of death-warning. Of those who live but are soon to die, he shall receive a vision and with his skill save those who perish unjustly afore their time."

"A worthy skill, one Grandfather had. Will my sons seek the ones they're mated too when they come of age, as Gilleoin did with me?"

"Aye, that alone is in their shifter blood, as is the ability to merge minds with the one their soul cries out for. When your sons reach the age of twenty, their soul shall lead them to their mate, the full moon guiding them to their chosen one. To join in all ways, they will need to complete the bond and forge the unbreakable merge of the mind as Gilleoin did with you."

Such relief rolled through Sorcha. "Where shall they find their mates?"

"Your eldest shall remain here, his chosen one from our village along the loch. She, like you and I, is part fae. She will bear him many bairns, and with the infusion of her fae blood into your eldest son's line, 'twill also ensure our people's fae skills will remain strong in his offspring. Your youngest son though will travel far from this place in search of his chosen one. When he finds her, they will join and their line shall be shifter alone. Your youngest son will grow from strength to strength as chief of his own clan, a mighty leader who will draw the respect of all his people." Nessa stroked her forehead and pushed back her damp hair. "'Tis time for you to push, my dear. Your bairns cannae wait any longer."

"Nay. I must wait for Gill—" Pain surged through her and she cried out and bore down.

She pushed with all that was within her. At the end of the bed, her midwife crouched between her legs and caught her firstborn son as he slid free from her body. The babe let out a mighty cry as her midwife handed her son into her mother's waiting arms.

Nessa carried her grandson to the wide basin on top of the side table, settled him within the warm water and bathed him. Then carefully, she marked the side of her firstborn's neck and wiped the blood from the mark, one which took the shape of a bear's claw ringed by a star. "This claw-and-star mark," her mother said, "will symbolize your firstborn's dual shifter-fae blood."

"A worthy mark for the 'Son of the Bear.'"

"Aye, it is. What shall you name him?" Mother wrapped her crying babe in Gilleoin's Matheson plaid and with him swaddled in her arms, carried him to her.

She held her son and cupped his precious cheek as he gazed at her with striking golden eyes. His aura shimmered so profoundly, the most glorious pure white threaded with heavenly strands of gold. "I shall name him Kenneth, for he carries the divine skills of our fae people in his blood, just as his descendants will do." Each strand of gold in his aura gave proof his progeny would be strongly fae-skilled shifters, just as Mother had said.

"A most worthy name." Nessa took Kenneth from her, kissed his forehead and whispered to him, "You've also been given your late grandfather's name, and he would be honored if he knew." A soft expression crossed Mother's face as she glanced at her. "My dear, 'tis time to push again. Your second son desires to join his brother. The two dinnae care to be parted."

More pain. Her belly tightened and she thrust her elbows into the mattress, bore down and pushed. Her second son wailed with a hearty cry as he emerged and the midwife lifted him up for her to see. Fair hair, just like his elder brother had. So too he had the most stunning golden eyes—shifter eyes. His aura, so pure and white held a tinge of sizzling red around the edges, just as Gilleoin's did. Aye, he was shifter alone and so too his descendants would be. "I shall call him Ivan, for he shall be gifted with strength and wisdom. He shall become a man of great honor when he is called to lead his own clan."

Mother returned Kenneth to the crook of Sorcha's right arm then took Ivan from the midwife and bathed him.

"I shall mark your youngest son as well, but only with the

bear's claw to symbolize his shifter blood alone. This mark will grace his line." Gently, she marked the side of her second-born son's neck and wiped the blood away. The singular bear's claw was perfect. Nessa wrapped him in a plaid and rocked him in her arms then carefully settled Ivan within Sorcha's other arm.

Sorcha cradled her sons to her chest, right next to her heart, where they would forever remain. "I've longed for this day, when I would hold you both in my arms. I love ye, as greatly as I love your father."

Mother's eyes filled with tears and one trickled free. "My dear, I must impart to you all I've seen, and you must ensure your sons never forget the prophecy I'm about to speak of." Nessa's aura shimmered like that of sparkling stars, reflecting her divine honesty and her great seer ability.

"Speak of what you've seen. I will hear it all." Her mother's prophecies, so strong and true, were never to be taken lightly. She would hold whatever words were spoken close to her.

Hands lifted high, Nessa's wise eyes clouded over. *"Gilleoin's sons will separate when they come of age and rule their own clans, yet there will come a time far in the future when a mated bond forms between the two clans. Only then must Gilleoin's descendants once again merge, and the 'power of three' be unveiled."* She opened her eyes and blinked the haze away.

"Why must their descendants once again merge?" Sorcha brushed a kiss over Kenneth and Ivan's brows.

"If they dinnae, then both Kenneth and Ivan's lines shall be like the leaves that fall from the trees. They will scatter too far and wide then turn to dust, and in doing so, their shifter race will be no more."

"Sorcha!" Gilleoin rushed into her chamber, shirttails fluttering over his kilt and his claymore bobbing within the baldric holstered across his broadly muscled back. He stumbled to her bedside, his golden eyes wide. "My love, you've birthed our bairns?"

"Aye, ye missed their arrival. Meet Kenneth and Ivan."

"Are ye well? Are they well?" He wrapped his arms around her and their sons. "They are such wee things."

"We're very well, and Mother had a vision. Both our sons

shall hold your ability to shift, and the eldest, Kenneth, also holds my people's fae skills."

"Such a blessing." He kissed her then grinned at his sons. "This day our clan shall celebrate a new beginning."

Aye, a new beginning she would treasure to the depths of her soul, for Gilleoin was now no longer alone. His sons would lead with strength and determination, just as their father led their clan. The heart of the bear would beat strongly within them both.

Chapter 1

Matheson Castle, Scotland, current day.

Isla Matheson gripped the stone windowsill of the briefing room as the dawn's rising sun sent a blaze of yellow and pink shimmering across the treetops and the glassy stillness of the loch. The forest stretched for miles either side of Matheson Castle, providing their shifter-fae skilled clan descended from Kenneth's line with the perfect level of isolation they needed from the rest of the world. That isolation though would never keep her bear shifter mate, a man born to the other clan—Ivan's line—from finding her, not when his senses reared to life when the full moon rose. This was the one night she both feared and desired. For five long years, she'd run, attempting to keep one step ahead of her mate's relentless pursuit. He was strong, but then again so was she.

"I thought I'd find you in here." The door to the briefing room shut with a soft snick and her father walked in with a laptop wedged under one arm. Murdock Matheson was both a seer and the chief of their clan, her only parent and one she loved dearly.

"I just needed a quiet place to gather my thoughts. The full moon looms."

"Speaking of the full moon. I have some new information about your shifter mate." He laid one hand on her shoulder and gave a gentle squeeze. "Are you prepared to listen?"

"Always. Did you have a vision?"

"I did, and from that vision I was able to discover exactly who he is."

"I already know who he is."

"You only know he's from Ivan's line."

"That's all I need to know. He's not from our clan and I'm worried about being the one who sets the prophecy in motion, as well as anxious about losing you." At least the other Matheson clan kept their location as tightly a guarded secret as they did theirs. Even during those times of the month when the desperate need to join with him rode her hard, she couldn't.

"You're in pain and I can see it. Running from your chosen one is difficult. This is a bond that runs to the depths of one's soul, whether you've met him or not." He set his laptop down on the large mahogany table in the center of the room and wrapped one arm around her shoulders. *"Gilleoin's sons will separate when they come of age and rule their own clans, yet there will come a time far in the future when a mated bond forms between the two clans. Only then must Gilleoin's descendants once again merge, and the 'power of three' be unveiled."* He breathed slowly out. "Yours is the first mated bond to form between the two clans in over eight-hundred years and whether you wish it or not, Gilleoin's lines must once again merge."

"I can't leave you, no matter if I want him." Damn the strength of the mated bond and its unearthly pull on her. She didn't want to leave her father. She was all he had. He needed her.

"Yet your future has been set, and I can't continue keeping you all to myself, even as much as I would love to." He pressed a kiss to her forehead. "Let me show you what I've uncovered. This is footage taken by a city surveillance camera I was able to download."

"If you believe I need to see it then please, show me." With her heart torn in two, she walked to the table, prepared to face her future even as she ran from it.

"I'll hook this up to the big wall screen." In his navy trousers and tan button-down shirt, Dad powered up his laptop, keyed in a sequence and moments later, the high definition floor-to-ceiling TV screen on the far wall, lit up a solid blue then flashed to the first image.

A city street. The glass front doors of a bank opened and a tall man with shoulder-length locks of midnight-black strode out. A tattooed mark, in the shape of a bear's claw on the side of his neck, gave evidence of exactly who he was. Only the chief's eldest son within Ivan's line—the second-born son—held that mark.

She palmed her dual claw-and-star tattoo hidden low on her

hip under her jeans. As her father's only daughter, his only child, he'd marked her with the firstborn's mark. She lifted her gaze. The man on the screen strode along the pavement, his black pants hugging his muscled legs and his white collared shirt stretching tight across his broad shoulders. His bearing and imposing height ensured those walking toward him veered out of his way, then he slowed and stopped next to a sleek red convertible. He opened the door, his long sleeves lifting and exposing the tip of a sheathed wrist dagger.

A slow heat invaded her limbs and spread in a rippling wave through her body. This kind of reaction to her chosen one, she didn't need. "What's his name?"

"Iain, the eldest son of Michael Matheson, the chief of his clan."

"Where's their shifter base located?"

"That I haven't unearthed yet, and last night when I called my government contact, he informed me he couldn't disclose that information, just as he couldn't disclose our location to the other clan." They'd been aware for some time that the other clan worked the same high level government cases that they did. "Although I was informed that your mate has put in several requests demanding further information on us. Of course he's been denied each time."

"He's impatient."

"I'd say he's done trying to track you on the night of the full moon. You're too fast, too quick at running."

"Running is the pits." That tore at her the worst, knowing what she denied them both. The mated pairs within her clan held the closest bond and she'd always desired the same, to be so at one with the man who wished to be the same with her. If only her mate wasn't from Ivan's line it would make all the difference. She didn't want to give up her father or her people. "That sweet ride of his should be easy enough to track via satellite if we go back through that day's images. We don't need to rely on our contact."

"You wish to know where he lives?"

"Aye, so I can stay well away from the place."

"I've already done a search. Iain waited it out at a hotel then traveled under the shield of darkness once he left the city.

They're as secretive as we are and remain well under the radar."

"What else have you got on him?" Her father never left any stone unturned once he began an investigation.

"Iain is a triplet and has two brothers, both identical. I discovered that information while searching through the births records. That's where I discovered his father's name and designation."

On the screen, Iain scanned his surroundings then stopped and stared at the surveillance camera mounted near the bank. Gaze narrowed, he looked right at her, his stunning golden eyes shimmering in the sunlight. She could drown in that gaze. So beautiful. Her fingers tingled and she itched to grab him, to remove the space that separated them by the camera lens. "He's definitely my mate. My desire for him is strong."

Slowly, she stepped around the table and stopped before the screen. She lifted one hand, traced along the firm angle of his jaw and over his bottom lip. His tongue darted out, his heated gaze turning to one of promise before he stepped back, eased inside his car, revved the engine and took off with a squeal across the blacktop. Gone, and everything within her cried out at the loss. "It'll be harder to steer clear of him now I've seen his image."

"You've been struggling lately regardless."

"Which city, Dad?"

"Edinburgh, although he could be anywhere by now." He turned his laptop off and the wall-mounted screen went blank. "There's no taming an alpha male's bear, Isla. He's closing in on you and I can sense that."

"There's no taming a compeller either." She was Murdock Matheson's daughter, a fae gifted shifter who held a hypnotic voice none could ignore. She'd confront her mate only as and when she was ready.

"Just remember, your ability to sense him tonight will be different now you've seen him."

"Oh, I'm aware." A desire to tangle with her mate seared through her, left her both wanting and uneasy. She jiggled where she stood.

"I want you to relax." Dad stepped up to her, grasped her hands. "You also need to cease worrying so much about me.

Focus only on what you know is the right thing to do."

"I'll try, but old habits die hard." She hugged her father, the one man she loved beyond all reason.

* * * *

After leaving her father, Isla strode to her chamber, opened her desk drawer and palmed her gun. Their work was dangerous no matter the skills they held and even though she'd be on the run tonight, before that time she had an active case to work with her partner, Daniel. Owen and Ewan Mathie were two shifters within a rogue offshoot Matheson branch, one that thankfully held a very weakened bloodline. Those two men, brothers of the same ilk, had killed two innocent people on the night of the last full moon when they'd allowed their bears to roam and now that they'd tasted human blood, they had to be captured and contained. She looked forward to the chase, to ensuring they paid for their crime. It'd certainly take her mind off her mate's chase tonight.

Swiftly, she slid her weapon into the back rise of her blue jeans then strapped on her ankle dagger and tugged her favorite knee-high black leather boots over the top. She swapped her long-sleeved shirt for a cooler white tank top since summer sat on the brink of arrival and her shifter-fae blood ran hotter than mere human blood alone.

Strappy red purse slung over her shoulder, she opened the door to find Daniel leaning against the opposite wall. "You appear ready to roll."

"Just waiting on you." He slung his battered denim jacket over one shoulder and pushed off the wall, his disheveled blond hair falling forward over his brow. "I can't wait to capture the Mathies."

"Me too." She trod down the passageway beside him. "I saw on the latest data that came in that we're heading to Loch Bear."

"To the bed and breakfast right on the fringes of the forest. It's the only place where the Mathies might stay that's close enough to their last known location. Have you got your sweet voice primed in readiness?"

"I do. What about Emma? Will you be able to make it back in time to spend the night with her?" His wife and her best friend had given birth six weeks ago to the first cub conceived in their clan in five years. They were all completely besotted with the wee boy who had the sweetest tuft of blond hair and the most stunning golden eyes. If only their clan births weren't dismally down. It made her decision to run from her mate all the more harder since she was adding to the problem of their people's slow extinction instead of aiding it.

"Emma understands."

"I highly doubt it." Their desire for their chosen one intensified beyond control on this one magical night. It was when their bears rode them the hardest.

"Well, she understands enough to let me go. I also intend to return just as soon as I'm able to."

"When is her next medical checkup?" One of their clansmen held a medical degree and rooms on the first floor, his door always open.

"She's got an appointment today. We're both hoping she'll get the all-clear. Her bear is clawing for its release." A female couldn't shift while carrying a child or in the weeks following her cub's birth, not until her body was fully healed and the Change no longer harmful to one or both of them.

"I'll make sure to drop in and see her once we're back, that's if you let her out of your bedroom." She strolled downstairs then headed around the perimeter of the great hall. Near the fireplace, several of their clansmen lounged on a group of four comfy blue swede couches. She waved out but didn't stop to chat, not when they needed to be away. She stepped outside and strode down the front steps.

Across the keep, a dozen men had broken into groups of two and shirtless, wearing only low-slung jeans or their belted plaid, they battled each other with their swords and shields glinting in the midmorning sunshine. Modern technology had changed the world, but at the heart of their clan, they still adhered to the old ways. And with their shifter-fae blood so strong, the only way to expend their immense energy was with such intense training.

She followed the cobbled path around the side of the keep and walked through the postern gate. In the rear lot, the center's black SUVs lined up in a row, gleamed.

Daniel pulled a set of keys from his pocket and opened their vehicle. She hopped into the passenger seat while he turned the ignition on. The radio blared and she turned it down.

They drove along the winding road, left the sanctuary of Matheson land and joined the thrum of traffic on the main highway. This was the most beautiful land. Rolling fields of heather were awash with wildflowers and the craggy hills of the Highlands called to her very soul.

"Sooo," Daniel drawled, "his name is Iain Matheson."

"Dad told you?"

"I was there when he downloaded the footage. I'm also your partner. There's nothing you can't keep from me that I won't eventually ferret out."

"'Cause you're nosy like that." She smiled. In truth she kept nothing from Daniel and never had. They'd grown up together, tussled as cubs and still did as adults. "Now I need to decide what I do about tonight."

"You're thinking of doing something different to the norm?" Interest flared in his gaze. "You feeling the need to get laid, little sister?"

"Not if Iain Matheson is as annoying as you are to be around." She rested her arm along the armrest under the open window and tapped the black leather. "It's no wonder he's been so persistent. He's their chief's eldest son. I'm surprised he didn't actually find me that first night." She'd waited out in the courtyard, so hopeful that when her mate appeared, she'd be overcome by the bond and finally be able to join with the one man who'd always been meant to be hers. Although none of her clansmen had appeared and that had rocked her soul, and her world.

"A lucky break for sure."

"What did you think of the footage?"

"He's one big bear, but if you need me to brawl with him, I can bring out the claws." His tone was smooth, his grin a teasing one.

"What claws? You keep levitating your opponents then just kick back while they twirl helplessly around in the air."

"Iain's no fae-skilled shifter. I'd have to even the playing field with him and set my ability aside. It'd be the only right thing to do."

"You are all talk." She laughed and squeezed his arm. "There's a very good chance should I ever allow my good sense to fly out the window and let my mate capture me, that I'd get real feisty with you for playing with what's mine. I might even have to take you down."

"You couldn't take me down if you tried."

"Wanna bet?"

"Five bucks says I'm right. I bet I could take your mate down and you wouldn't even lift a finger to help him."

"One hundred bucks says I'm right and you're the one going down."

"I'll stretch to ten but that's it."

"You're clearly worried I'll win. One hundred and not a cent less."

"Fine. I was just trying to save you some money for when you lose."

"Sure you were." More of her tension seeped from her. Daniel knew how to divert her thoughts and lighten her mood.

"Have I ever mentioned how much Emma likes being levitated?" That teasing grin of his was back in place. "I spin her around and have my wicked way as I—"

"No." She flung up a hand. "Too much information."

"Wimp." He chuckled as he motioned toward the gas station up ahead. "I'll pull over here and refuel while you grab us some lunch." He indicated then crawled into the far lane once it had cleared.

She strolled inside, perused the café area with its shelved delicacies and drooled over the offerings. She had a mighty sweet tooth and selected two slices of gooey chocolate cake as well as half a dozen sandwiches to share between them, of which Daniel would eat the lion's share. He always did. Where he packed all the food he consumed though, she had no idea. With two cups of steaming coffee in hand, black and strong, she trod back to her partner and passed him his brew.

He drove and they munched and planned their coming mission. The weakened offshoot Mathie branch only held four shifters and Owen and Ewan could only shift on the night of the full moon, which meant tonight was the night they had to catch them if they wished to ensure another innocent person wasn't harmed.

Hours passed and Daniel weaved along the winding forest road while along the horizon, the sun began its descent. "You need to hurry it up," she told him.

"We're almost there." He eyed the GPS. "We'll make it before nightfall and before the Mathies have a chance to shift. We've got to catch them before they cause more mayhem."

"I've never been this far east before."

"I have, a time or two." He pointed up ahead at a quaint stone cottage nestled within the woods. "There's the inn we're after."

He slowed then pulled into the gravel parking lot. A sandstone cobbled path led to inn's front door with its rustic bed and breakfast sign strung above it. With one finger, Daniel lifted his aviator sunglasses up and surveyed the area. "Nice and remote. The untamed forest surrounding this place would definitely call to their bears."

"Then let's go rope us some big bear." She hopped out, patted her weapon still resting at her back and walked around to Daniel as he holstered his gun under his jacketed arm and straightened his buttery-colored t-shirt over his black pants.

At the hood, he breathed slowly out, his claws slicing in and out.

"You okay?"

"Just fighting the early stages of the full moon. I want my mate." The males always suffered to a greater degree on this one night, their need riding them hard if their female remained some distance away. It wouldn't help that it had been some time since they'd last been able to join as one.

"You got the sedative?" She nudged his arm.

"Sure do." He dug out two vials from his inner denim jacket pocket and gave the deep orange concoction a swirl. After they'd caught the Mathies, they'd ensure they slept until they'd dropped them off to their contact. Owen and Ewan would require containment unlike the rest of the criminal population. Daniel turned in a slow circle, this time sniffing the air.

She did the same.

A trace of smoke puffing from the inn's chimney added a

slight taint to the pine fresh air swirling around her. She dug deeper. Beneath the pine, she caught the deep earthy tones of the land. No bears.

She attuned her hearing. Small critters scampered through the dense underbrush and the splashing of water beyond, traveled to her with ease. "There's a river close by."

"But no bears. We'll need to check inside as well as do a wider perimeter search." He set a hand at her back and guided her past a scratched-up mustard-colored Jeep, a white van and a blue sedan.

At the front door, he pressed the bell and waited beside her.

"I'll see who that is." A man's deep voice rumbled through the door. It swung open and the portly gentlemen with a head of gray hair nodded at them. "Good evening, folks. Are you after a room for the night?"

"We are." Daniel slung an arm over her shoulders and ruffled her long hair. "My sister and I are heading up higher into the mountains in the morning. Do you have any vacancies?"

"The wife has her family staying over for a few days so we only have the one room left. It does have two single beds though, so it's yours if you'd like it."

"We heard." Isla cleared her throat and used her hypnotic voice to its fullest. "That you might have seen two men we're eager to catch up with. Both brothers, their names Owen and Ewan Mathie."

He stared into her eyes, his own clouding over under her compulsion. "They dropped in, and have twice before. They left not long ago to take a hike in the woods. That Jeep in the lot is theirs. They asked if they could leave it there for the night and I agreed. They wanted to sleep out under the stars tonight, although they used the spare room last night."

"Could you confirm that this is them?" She slid a photograph of Owen and Ewan from her pocket and passed it across.

"That's them all right."

Daniel sent her a silent look that said, *Bingo. Now let's find them.*

She smiled at the proprietor. "We'd like to take a look around. I'd appreciate it if you showed my brother the room the two men stayed in while I wander around the backyard. You'll find nothing suspicious about our request and you'll forget you ever saw us after we leave."

"Of course." His glazed eyes focused a little, but her compulsion would hold without issue for Daniel. No one had broken through her ability's hold yet.

She winked at her partner. "I'll take the outside since compelling beats levitation. Call out if you need my help."

"Sure will." He wandered inside with the proprietor.

Setting out, she trekked along the cobbled pathway winding around to the rear of the property. Either side of the walkway, thick lavender bushes swayed in the breeze. She stepped onto the grass dotted with tiny yellow flowers and surveyed the area. The forest butted right up to the rear of the property. She marched in that direction and finally caught the very faintest whiff of bear. Excitement thrummed through her and she picked up her pace and entered the woods. Jogging, she followed the leaf-strewn trail into the dark recesses of the wild. Her bear pushed under her skin, demanding the Change. "Not yet," she urged it. "You've got to wait until our job is done."

Ahead, the trees stood tall and proud next to a fast-moving river and two massive bears clawed a trunk then sniffed, jerked their gazes toward her and snarled.

"Well, hello, boys. I take you two are Owen and Ewan? It's about time we met."

They shoved off the trunk and landed heavy on all fours. Both prowled toward her, their beady black eyes holding only the barest rim of shifter gold on the edges. They heaved up onto their hind legs and roared, drool flying from their jaws.

"Down!"

They bellowed and attempted to fight her compulsion.

"I said—"

A man bounded out of the brush, slung her over his shoulder and bolted along the trail through the trees. Branches scraped her bare arms and her hair flew into her face and obscured her vision.

She shoved her hair back and clutched his pumping arms, her belly thumping into his rock hard shoulder. The ground blurred and the trees whizzed by. She couldn't catch her breath.

"W-what are you doing?"

"Getting you far away from those bears." One deeply sensual tone that curled her toes. Now that really shouldn't be happening.

Everything spun and she squeezed her eyes shut. "I can't leave my partner to fight those bears on his own." She shoved her upper body up, looped her arms around his neck and slid down his chest and into his arms. "I want you to—" Whoa. Her heartbeat tripped out of time.

Oh hell. Her mate had found her, and the moon only just glimmered on the horizon.

* * * *

Iain Matheson couldn't believe his good fortune. He'd been out in the woods close to Ivanson Castle when he'd scented her, the one woman he'd been searching five long years for. His bear had gone half-crazy with need and so had he. He only wished he'd been paying more attention to his surroundings. He'd missed catching the other two unknown shifters as they'd made the Change so close by, shifters not of his clan, of that he was sure.

"I—I—" She searched his gaze then blinked as if checking to make sure he was real. "Put me down." Her voice rang with authority, with a sweetly hot demand that curled around his senses, a demand he couldn't ignore.

Gently, he lowered her to her feet, set her before him. A compeller. This wouldn't be easy.

"I see you hold one of the rarest of the fae skills." He'd scoured through what historical information remained on record, even as scarce as it was. Being aware of what he might be up against when he did find his mate, had been a necessity.

"I do." Her golden eyes, so gloriously alive, flickered with defiance and frustration. He'd need to take great care to ensure she didn't use her skill against him. Now that he'd finally found her, he didn't care to lose her. Or at least not before he knew exactly where she lived.

"You've been very hard to track down." Hard was an understatement. If only his clan held the knowledge of where the original House of Clan Matheson resided, but when Ivan had left his home, so many centuries ago, so too he'd taken the knowledge of their location and kept it from even one soul. Arms crossed, he listened for any movement through the woods. Not one noise, other than the chirping of birds and buzzing of nighttime insects. "You said you can't leave your partner to fight those bears alone. Who's your partner and who were those shifters? They're trespassing on my clan's land."

"Owen and Ewan Mathie. They're brothers who are predators through and through, and must be stopped, tonight, before they can harm another. I left my partner behind. Daniel won't be happy that I did." Her cell phone jingled and she hauled it from her jeans pocket, pressed the speaker and answered. "Daniel, the Mathies are in the forest, about a quarter of a mile to the north of the inn."

"Not anymore they're not. I chased them, but then they backtracked to the inn and took off in their Jeep, right after they slashed one of our tires. I'm changing it now. I'll never be able to catch them with the head start they've got. Where are you?"

"With Iain." She eyed him, sexy narrowed gaze and all.

"Well, that would explain why you left me in such a hurry. Can't control your little bear, eh?"

"She's contained, but my mate isn't."

"You owe me a hundred bucks, Miss You-can't-play-with-my-bear."

"You're not even here for me to stop your bout of playing."

"That makes no difference. You removed him from my field of play."

"He removed me."

"You still lost." A clanking sounded down the line as if her partner had dropped a wrench. Daniel grunted. "Stupid sucky tire. I've almost got it changed."

"Where do you want to go from here, Daniel?" Isla asked him.

"I'll update the chief and form a plan. For now, you do what you need to and we'll talk again in the morning. I'm not leaving here until I know exactly where we need to head. We'll contain the Mathies, one way or another, and soon. Very soon."

"I'll talk to you first thing, or call me sooner if you need to."

"Wait." Iain seized her hand before she could hang up and

memorized the numbers on the screen, both hers and her partner's. "I'll talk to you tomorrow too, Daniel."

She glared at him and hung up before Daniel could answer. "You've really tossed a spanner in the works."

"Lovely to meet you too."

"Don't try and be funny." She muttered under her breath as she tucked her phone away then paced the trail in front of him. Softly, she sighed and stopped. "I'm sorry. I'm not normally so rude. It's just this isn't the way I ever envisioned meeting you, and right now I'm currently frustrated. I don't mean to push that frustration onto you." She blew out a long breath then extended her hand. "The name's Isla."

"Nice to meet you, Isla. I'm Iain." He slid his fingers around hers, her skin so warm and soft. Releasing her hand took a whole lot of effort. "Would you care to take a walk? Have a chat and all?"

"It'd be a nice start. Thank you."

"We'll follow the trail." He set a hand at her back and steered her along it. The last rays of the sun shimmered across the darkening sky then disappeared. The full moon hung heavy and low within a blanket of black, its brightness lighting their path along with a glittering array of stars. "I apologize for making you lose your catch. I wasn't aware we had rogue bears on our land."

"Catching them is Daniel's and my current assignment." Her gaze softened as she looked at him. "Honestly, I'm sorry I was so abrupt. I try not to be rude to people I've just met."

"I surprised you. That's clear to see. Tell me a little about yourself."

"Not much to tell. I'm as elusive as they come."

He needed more information than that, and he intended to push as hard as she'd let him. "Have you got any family?"

"Of course. Apart from my entire clan, I have a father. He's the chief and seer of my clan. Murdock Matheson. I'm his eldest, his one and only." She looked ahead along the trail. "You must live close by to have caught me this early on in the evening."

"It appears you've come straight to me this time. Ivanson Castle is just around the other side of Loch Bear."

"So I get to meet you and your entire clan at the same

time?"

"No, not if you don't wish to. Just me if that suits you best."

"Just you for now. That I can handle." She shivered as the breeze picked up. It blew her glossy brown locks about her bare shoulders and caused goose-bumps to rise on her arms.

"Here, allow me warm you up." He shrugged his jacket off and held it up for her to slip her arms into. She didn't hesitate to accept his offering. She pushed her hands into the long sleeves of soft black leather and pulled the front edges of his jacket together, covering the white tank top she wore over her jeans.

"Thank you. I wasn't expecting to go for such a long jaunt this deep into the forest." She lifted the collar over her nose and breathed deep. "Mmm, you smell good."

His bear had him leaning in. He buried his nose in her hair, dragged in her sweet vanilla scent. It swirled around and intoxicated him, made him want to pick her up and sling her back over his shoulder all over again. Instead, he gently rubbed her arms then zipped his jacket up and enclosed her completely within its warmth. "Feeling a little less frustrated now?"

"A touch less." She slanted her head, her gaze questioning. "I have no intention of leaving my clan, even though you've found me."

"Is that why you've run from me all these years?"

"My clan's numbers are dwindling. There are far fewer mated pairs than ever before and when I discovered you weren't from my clan, I'd never felt such sorrow. I've let them down."

"So by running, you decided our fate before you'd even given me a chance to prove myself." He stroked a finger under her chin and his bear rumbled in delight at the sheer softness of her skin—so creamy and smooth. "I would never keep you from your kin, Isla, nor do I ever intend to in the future. There must be give and take between mates, and more so between you and I since we come from separate clans."

"You're serious?" Her tone held disbelief. "You won't insist I leave my people to join with you?" She inched closer, touching the tips of her boots to his. Those long legs of hers, encased in dark blue denim, showcased every delectable curve from her pert bottom to her knee-high leather boots that hugged her slim calves.

"That's right."

"Then I'm free to go?"

"You're free to leave whenever you wish, but if you go, then I go with you."

"There isn't a chance you'll abandon your clan to join mine. You're the eldest son of Ivan's line." She lifted one hand, traced her finger over the bear's claw on his neck.

"You seem to know more about me than I know about you, and I'll only ever speak the truth with you. I'd never leave my clan, but so too I'd never demand that you leave yours. I'm open to negotiation, to ensure we both receive what we need to from this bond. I'm not an enforcer with a steel hand."

"Is that right?" She arched one cute brow, rather teasingly.

His mate was feisty and strong, both qualities he admired in any woman, as well as qualities he'd hoped his chosen one held.

"And what is it you'd like to receive from this bond, my mate?"

"You. I desire the bond and all that it entails, but I want the sharing of lives, including that of our clans."

"I'm not really that great of a catch. I can be a little unruly, rash, indecisive, and a complete pain in the butt, or at least that's what Daniel always says. I'd be running in the other direction if I were you, and count yourself very lucky you got away."

"I'll never run in the opposite direction from you." Unable to help himself and needing some form of touch that was so important to shifters, he rested his hands on her hips. "There is a lot a man learns during the chase. You hold great strength, are incredibly smart and have completely captured my attention."

"Are you flirting with me, Iain Matheson?" She slid her hands over his. "Because if you are, I like it."

"You've already proven to me that you're dedicated to the ones you love by not wanting to leave them."

"You need to stop with the flowery words." She smiled, so beautifully it lit up her eyes.

He drew her closer, until if he bent one single inch, he'd be able claim her lips and the kiss he so strongly desired. "Tell me the first thing you've learnt about me during the chase."

"Yesterday, I discovered you visited the bank in Edinburgh and took off afterward in a very sweet red convertible. My father had a vision and captured some footage of you, the first I've ever seen. I've also had the chance to admire your very fine looking butt while swinging over your shoulder. I could still take you though, and knock you for six, and all with my voice alone."

"What else have you got?"

"You've got two brothers, both identical to you."

"And their names?"

"No idea. Tell me about your family." Her curiosity must be eating at her the same way it ate at him.

"My parents are mated, and my brothers and I are tight, very tight. Their names are Finlay and Kirk and we hold a brotherly bond that allows us to sense each other's feelings."

"Interesting." That cute eyebrow shot back up. "Are they mated?"

"They are, but like me, they still search for their chosen ones."

"Well, their chosen ones aren't from my clan. There aren't any more unmated females of the right age other than me, and I'm not the sharing kind of girl. I'm yours alone. What's their search been like?"

He almost purred at that declaration.

"Rather otherworldly. On the night of the full moon, they're led to where they sense their mate is, yet there is nothing and no one about."

"And they haven't given up their search?" She gripped the sides of his short-sleeved shirt, fisted the black cotton in her hands.

"Not once, and they never shall. The drive to find their women is too strong, as it has been for me." He pressed a kiss to the top of her head, needing an even deeper kind of touch, which would likely only get worse as the night continued on. "It's getting cold out. Let's keep walking."

"To your lair?"

"Aye, to my lair." He steered her along the winding upward trail, her pace slower than before, and not in a nervous don't-want-to-go-with-you kind of way, but as if she was more relaxed, or perhaps curious. Her attentive gaze kept switching from the trail ahead to him.

Before long, they left the trail behind and emerged before

Ivanson Castle, the thick stone walls of the keep rising like an impenetrable fortress in the dark. "This is the home of my ancestors and has been since Ivan's day. You also have my word you're free to go at any time, provided I go with you."

"I'm going to keep you to your word."

"My word is true, always has been and always will be." He gestured toward the two-story gatehouse where battlements topped fortified walls and cameras mounted on the top of each crenelated corner sent surveillance footage directly to the guards inside the control room. "Are you prepared to see where our bond shall lead us?"

"That all depends on what you expect from me tonight."

"All I desire is to get to know you. You've nothing to fear."

"It's not fear that rides me. This moment marks a huge change. Nothing will be as it was before the moon rose tonight." She touched her chest then his. "Do you feel it? Our bond already strengthens. I'm quite content to be around you, not nervous or hell bent on running in the least."

"I do feel it, and I promise we'll take whatever is to come, just one day at a time." He caught her hand, curled his fingers around hers and looked deep into her eyes. "I need you, Isla. Meeting you is all I've longed for."

"You seem far too agreeable." She searched his gaze then nodded. "All right. I can do this, but just you and me as promised. We'll talk some more, get a feel for each other and where we stand."

"Thank you." His mate was prepared to talk and for that he was most grateful.

He escorted her through the gates and across the inner courtyard toward the side entrance where they could bypass the great hall and surrounding rooms where his family would be. Through the darkened passageways, he led her then up the tower's side stairs and into his chamber. Quietly, he shut the door. "Take a seat. I'll have you warm in no time. There's an attached bathroom if you have need of it."

One with no window and only one door. He could safely allow her out of his sight when she had no means of escape. He'd meant it when he said she wouldn't be going anywhere without him.

"I'm fine for now, but thanks for the offer all the same."
She ambled across to his narrow window and with one finger,
parted the navy drapes and peered out. "What were you up to in
the city the other day?"

"I take care of the clan finances and such. Traveling to the
city is a regular jaunt, one you are always welcome to join me
on. I'd be sure to make it fun, in and amongst working the
figures and monitoring our land and stock holdings." On his
knees at the hearth, he tore bark from a log, removed his wrist
dagger and struck his flint then blew on the sparks. Flames
flickered and he tossed a block of peat on top. He snuck a look
over his shoulder when she continued to remain quiet. Her
watchful gaze moved about his chamber, took in his large fur-
covered bed then returned to him. "Ever been to the city?" he
asked her.

"I'm not a city kind of girl." She stepped closer, raised her
palms to the flames. "I prefer the wilds of the Highlands,
although I'm curious to learn exactly how you'd be sure to make
it fun for me?"

"You'd have to come to find out." He rose and dusted his
hands against his jeans. She didn't live in the city or the higher
populated area surrounding it. At least he had another question
answered. "How dangerous is your work?"

"I never leave on assignment without a team member,
which is usually Daniel. Even though our clansmen are highly
skilled, we never take the chance of losing one of our number."
She backed up and perched on the lid of his engraved wooden
trunk at the end of his bed. A glorious smattering of freckles
sprinkled across her cheeks and nose, made him itch to touch
them, to move closer and trace each one.

"Are you warming up?"

"Aye, I am. Thank you." She unzipped his jacket, folded
and laid it beside her. "I didn't even sense you close tonight, not
even one hint of a warning."

"You should never feel uneasy when you sense me close
by." Not liking the distance she'd created, he closed the gap
between them and crouched at her feet. "Has your father aided
you in eluding me all these years, being that he's a seer?"

"No, I've managed to elude you all on my own. I also

wasn't paying a great deal of attention on you tonight, not when my mind was on my current case." She lifted a hand, cupped his cheek. "Honestly, it's been a burden running from you, and I know my father had hoped I'd soon one day stop."

"Your father sounds like a man I'd like to meet." As much as he'd detested her need to run, he'd also admired her ability to keep one step ahead of him. No more though. Now it was time for them to join together, to complete the bond—when she was ready—and merge their lives into one. All he'd ever anticipated was finding his chosen one, and for their clans to finally have some much needed hope. "We have so much to talk about."

"We do."

His mind reached out, brushed against hers and found a solid barrier. A barrier he didn't care for. Pushing, trying to find a way in, he couldn't halt his mind from demanding the merge that would invariably allow him a constant link of communication to the one woman who was always meant to be his.

"I can feel that." She scrubbed a hand across her forehead and grimaced.

"I'm sorry. The need to forge a merged link with you is strong. Everything within me desires it, to be a part of you, to speak with you at ease, no matter where you are." He hauled his mind back. The last thing he wanted to do was to harm or cause her any pain. He slid one hand around the back of her head and gently drew her forward until their foreheads touched. Her warm breath whispered across his cheeks and calmed a little of his mind's need. "Has the pain receded?"

"It's going." She rubbed her forehead against his.

"Earlier you said you were your father's eldest, his one and only. What of your mother?"

"She passed away not long after I was born. I was schooled right alongside Daniel and a few other close friends within clan walls, my father close by."

"I'm sorry about your mother. That must have been terribly hard for you and your father to lose her so soon in life." His parents were rarely apart, found any great length of distance separating them difficult, no matter their merged link. They were each other's confidants, lovers, their one-and-only. A relationship he desired with all his heart. Her admittance also brought with it a great deal of understanding. She and her father must be tight.

"It's never easy for one who is mated to lose their other half. Dad's commitment to raising me though kept him from losing it. His clan also needed him, and we rely on his wise judgment and strength." She looked deep into his eyes. "I've always felt torn, Iain. He's given up so much to remain with me, and I've felt driven to give him the same commitment in return."

"You harbor guilt?"

"Guilt, and love, and kin. They're a powerful combination."

"For the past five years, I've ached for what could be and for what's always remained just beyond my grasp. But I want you to lay any guilt you feel aside. Going forward, we start fresh, with no recriminations or blame. There is only us, and how we intend to live our lives from this moment forth." Being with her was all he'd longed for, and now the chance was here, he wasn't about to lose her before he'd ever had the chance to know her. "Apart from your father, who's your next closest?"

"Daniel."

"Does he have a mate?" The man better have.

"Aye, and a wee son who is only six weeks old. Daniel holds the fae skill of telekinesis. With his mind alone, he can levitate objects or people."

"Then I thank you for the warning." He didn't doubt that as close kin, Daniel would be as protective of Isla as her father would be.

"You'll need the warning, although I'd never let Daniel hurt you." She touched one fingertip to his chest then slid it between two of his shirt buttons and stroked his skin. "You're very warm, almost too warm."

"It's been a few days since I last shifted. Being in the city prevented me from doing so and when I returned, I was busy preparing for the chase."

"If you need to shift now, feel free to do so."

"I'll only shift if you do."

She shook her head. "I want to talk to you and I can't do that if I shift."

A good sign. His bear settled at the thought.

"Every mated pair in my clan knew each other for years before the mated bond drew them together." She popped another of his buttons, eased her entire hand fully inside and palmed his flesh. "We don't have that same benefit going into our mated bond. I don't want to move too fast, even though I can't help but want to touch you. The need is strong."

"As it is for me, and we'll take things as slow as you need to. We'll find the right balance. I like having your hands on me. It's soothing." It calmed him as nothing else could. "Touch me, wherever and however you please."

"You are far too amenable."

"I've never made the offer to another soul, just you." He rested his hands on her hips, slid his thumbs under the hem of her white tank top and stroked her smooth skin. "And if I move too fast, rein me back in. I'll understand." Gazing into her eyes, he shared the words emblazoned deep on his heart. "What belongs to me is now yours, including all that I am."

"You are also far too sexy for words." A teasing smile lifted her lips. "Does that inclusion of what belongs to you go as far as your convertible?"

"The key is in the top drawer of my dresser and the car is parked in the lot out the back. You have to take the postern gate to reach it, but again, you're not to leave without me. That is my one and only stipulation." He caressed her back and pressed her closer. Five years of searching for her, of feeling incomplete and now she was here, right where she belonged. He closed his eyes as another wave of deep desire rushed through him. "Thank you for allowing this kind of touch. I need it, bad."

"The urge to bond is strong." She lifted her arms and wrapped them around his neck. "The full moon is attempting to get its way."

"We'll control what will or won't happen this night, not the moon." He sank his hands into her hair and luxuriated in the slide of her dark silky locks slipping across his wrists and forearms. His bear fairly purred for more and carefully, he unleashed a touch of his control, lifted her up, scooted with her onto his bed and laid down beside her, one leg firmly over hers to hold her in place.

"Talking of control." She touched her lips to his ear and

whispered, "Stay very still. No more moving for you."
Hypnotically compelling words.

"You don't need to compel me if you don't wish for me to
move." Damn it. He couldn't move a muscle. She'd restrained
him, fully and completely. "How often do you use your skill?"

"When and as needed, but I just couldn't help myself right
now." She nudged him onto his back and perched beside him
then lifted one foot and unzipped her boot. She tossed it onto the
floor then unzipped the other.

"How long does the compulsion last?"

"Do you mean when will you be able to move?"

"Exactly."

"Until I free you." She winked, shuffled to the end of the
bed and unlaced his boots. She removed and propped them next
to hers then crawled back up and straddled his hips. With one
sensual move, she slid a weapon from the back rise of her jeans,
checked the safety and leaning over him, placed it on the bedside
table.

His fingers twitched, the bone-deep need to touch her
clawing at him.

"Don't try to fight the compulsion. It can become painful if
you do."

"At least you're making yourself comfortable and not
racing out the door." Thank heavens for that.

"I just needed a moment, and you did say I could touch you,
wherever and however I pleased. I do tend to take things
literally." She traced along his lower lip, reached the center then
swept back to the corner. Her golden gaze swirled with desire,
the same fierce emotion raging through him. "When I first saw
your image from the footage my father downloaded from the
city, I touched you just like this." She stroked along his lip again
and he nipped her finger then sucked it inside his mouth. Slowly,
she leaned in, her lips a mere breath from his. "If you're in any
pain, then tell me."

A surge of heat flared down his spine, rolled into his groin
and hardened his cock. He groaned as his shaft rose and tried to
spear through his pants. "Ignore that."

"I've been celibate my entire life. I couldn't ignore any part
of you if I tried." She stroked down his chest and along his

waistband. "Would you like to move?"

"You compelled me for a reason, and not just to see how I managed not being able to move. I obviously came on too fast. I won't have you fear me or my touch in any way. If this is what you need to do to feel more comfortable, then I can readily accept it."

"I'm not uncomfortable, not in the least." She pressed one hand to his chest, right over his heart. "I want your touch, Iain. I want to get to know you, to see what I've been missing out on since the chase began. I know my father would want that for me too. I release you from your compulsion."

Even though she had, he remained perfectly still, his greatest desire now to unravel each and every intriguing part of her.

* * * *

Iain didn't move even though she'd released him from her compelling command. She smiled. "I like you. You've surprised me at each and every turn so far tonight."

"I like you too. I also want to smother you in my scent. Is that permissible?"

"Of course." Her heartbeat picked up its pace. She wanted his scent all over her, for both her and her bear. She couldn't hold back that need.

Gently, Iain rolled her onto her side then facing her, smoothed one hand over her lower back. Fingers splayed wide, he rubbed his body against hers, ensuring his scent encased her, just as he'd done outside in the forest when he'd slid his jacket off and zipped her securely within it. She liked it. A lot. Particularly when he slid his fingers underneath her shirt's hem and stroked along her waist.

She nuzzled his neck, right over his tattoo. "Your mark is stunning."

"Do you have any distinguishing marks yourself?"

"I'm the first female in my line to receive one." She lifted her tank top a touch and nudged her jeans down an inch to expose her hip and the small tattoo of the claw-and-star mark symbolizing her dual shifter-fae blood. "Since my mother passed away only a week following my birth and my father knew I'd be his only child, he honored me with the mark."

"It's beautiful." He stroked one thumb over it.

"Thank you." She tucked her top back down and played with the last two remaining buttons holding his shirt together.

"Take my shirt off if you wish."

"Are you reading my mind?" She desperately wanted to. Skin to skin contact was necessary between mated pairs and she was no different in her desires even though she'd run from him.

"I'd like nothing more than to read your mind, but it'll keep."

"You're doing a fine job even without the merged link." She lengthened one claw and sliced the buttons away then peeled the soft cotton back and licked her lips. His wide chest, so heavily muscled held a smattering of hair, the same dark shade as his head and a teasing trail led down and disappeared inside the waistband of his black jeans. She shoved his shirt off his shoulders, exposed his muscled arms and thick biceps. So beautiful, and all hers.

"Isla." He groaned, his golden gaze heating to a molten hue. "You may need to compel me again. Your touch is only going to encourage me to want more."

"What kind of 'more' would you like?"

"I want to kiss you."

"A kiss would be nice." She didn't want to turn him away, not when she too craved what she'd been forced to give up for so long.

"Then I have your permission?"

"You do."

He dipped his head, licked her lower lip then grinned. "You taste good."

"That's all you want?"

"Hell no." He covered her mouth with his and licked her tongue. She swayed forward and he captured her lips in a deliciously scorching kiss, his hard body a powerful heat that carved warmth into her own. Mmm, he tasted good, so good. She melted against him, reveling in his scent as it swirled around and embedded itself deep within her.

Even as she'd run from this bond, she'd still yearned for it. She melted further into his touch. His breath whispered softly across her tongue, an incredibly sensuous caress that had her urging his lips apart and deepening their kiss to capture more of his essence.

This was so very right, and she indulged as her need for more rushed through her. She plunged her tongue inside his mouth and drank in his delectable taste, welcoming the raw intimacy she'd never experience with another. Only him. He was the one destined to be hers. "Oh goodness." She pulled back a touch. "I really love the way you kiss."

"And I love the way you respond." He caressed her sides, roamed down and scooped her bottom. Then he kissed her again, so deeply, so wildly, that their breath mingled as one and completely scattered her thoughts.

"More, Iain."

"What kind of more do you want?"

"For you to mark me."

"Are you sure?"

"Very sure."

He rolled her onto her back and rose over top of her. He nibbled along her jaw and down her neck. She arched into his touch as he scraped his teeth over the sensitive skin where her neck and shoulder met.

A scorching heat shimmered through her and pooled between her thighs. She wanted his mark, just as she wanted to give him hers. "Do it."

"I'm just enjoying the ride leading up to it." He slid one finger under her shoulder strap and eased her tank top away from her neck. A low rumble vibrated in his chest as he pressed himself against her and sucked on her offered skin. Then he teased her with his tongue, stroked one hand down her throat, over her chest and curved his palm around her breast.

"I can't wait any longer." Her pulse raced, so fast.

"Neither can I." He bit down and arousal hit her hard and fast. She clutched his shoulders, her nails digging into his flesh.

He licked her skin, soothing the spot where he'd bitten before lifting his head and looking into her eyes. "Are you all right? Your skin is so flushed."

"I liked it, a lot."

"As did I." He rolled her into his side and pulled her tight against him, his hand firm on her thigh as he tucked his top leg between hers and ensured they touched along their entire length. Slowly, he slid her hair back from her shoulder and eased her other top strap to the side.

"Are you going to bite me again?"

"Aye, the same time you're going to bite me. Since completing our bond must wait, we both need this." Head lowered, he cupped the back of her head and drew her mouth to his neck. "Am I right? Tell me if I'm not."

"You're right." She gave into the deep need burning within her, sucked his skin into her mouth and razzed his flesh with her teeth. Her nipples hardened into tight points and she rubbed her breasts against his chest to ease the ache.

"Now," he growled.

She clamped down on him and he did the same to her. Pleasure coursed through her, sweeping her away on a tide of wonder. He was hers and she wanted everyone to know it, and this mark she'd given him would ensure it.

"Isla." He hissed out a breath and rocked his leg between hers.

"So good," she murmured, a tight need for more building deep inside her.

"What do you want? Tell me and I'll deliver."

"Make—got to have—I just need more."

"I've got you." He gripped her thigh, pressed his jean-clad leg even higher into her crotch and urged her to move on him. Sweet heaven. The seam of her jeans pressed into her clit and she couldn't help but rub harder against him.

Dizzy and breathless, she kissed him, with all the passion and intensity taking her over and he rocked his leg harder into her and made her gasp as white-hot pleasure struck her. It ricocheted outward from her core and hardened her nipples even further. He'd driven her so swiftly and completely over the edge and she soared as bright lights sizzled behind her closed eyelids. "Oh goodness," she panted as she slowly came back down. "That was totally unexpected."

* * * *

"It was also beautiful to see." Iain stroked Isla's hair as her breathing returned to normal. Watching her soar skyward from an orgasm he'd given her had made him deliriously happy. She was so responsive to his touch and he adored it. He nuzzled her neck, her scent below sweeping up and over him. So intoxicating. "Are you all right?"

She opened her eyes, blinked and cleared her dazed gaze. "I can't believe you just made me come, while I'm still fully clothed." She rubbed the spot where he'd bitten her in a slow circle with her thumb then palmed the mark and held it to her. "No more biting me tonight. I'm not sure I can handle another episode like that without wanting to tear your clothes off you."

"That was hardly a warning if that was your intention." His cock throbbed for release. He'd never had sex before, but he'd certainly watched a few interesting movies and right now all he wanted to do was slide her jeans down her legs and feast on that part of her that had wept for him.

"I can see what you're thinking." She tapped his nose. "You need to stop it."

"You're torturing me." He cupped her face in his hands and kissed her, his mouth moving in a slow exploration that left them both ragged for breath when he pulled back. It would take every ounce of his willpower not to succumb to this desperate desire he had for her tonight.

It would surely be one long evening.

One he never wanted to have end.

He'd found his mate and his soul rejoiced in the fact.

"Tell me what you're thinking," she murmured.

"My soul is in heaven."

"Likely right alongside mine after what you just did to me."

"Aye, what happens to you, happens to me." He grinned, completely taken by the woman before him. The days ahead shone with a brilliance he couldn't wait to explore. With her. Only with her.

Chapter 2

Twenty years following Kenneth and Ivan's birth, the ancient House of Clan Matheson, 1210.

The moon, golden and so very full, hung low over the loch and sent its blaze of warmth across the castle and forest beyond. Sorcha tucked her hand inside Gilleoin's as Kenneth and Ivan stood strong beside them. This night she'd lose one son even as she gained a daughter and so many emotions warred within her. Loss, sadness, yet also wonder and hope. 'Twas time for her sons to seek out their mates and claim them, to live the lives they were born for.

"All will be well, my love." Gilleoin kissed the top of her head. "This is a night of celebration, and we will no' consider it otherwise." He clasped his youngest son's shoulder. "Ivan, do you sense your mate?"

"Aye, I'm driven toward the east. She is far away, so distant 'twill take some time to reach her and with only this night of the full moon to guide me in the right direction."

"Nessa warned you that 'twould be so. This night though will set you on the right course."

"I will find her. Our souls are bound and I willnae be able to rest until I am with her."

Sorcha stepped forward. "Ivan, dinnae forget what your grandmother has also asked of you."

"To never disclose the location of this keep. I gave her my word I wouldnae. My descendants willnae merge again with my brother's line until the time for the prophecy to unveil arrives." He seized his father's forearms in a firm hold. "An adventure awaits." He released Gilleoin and hauled her into his arms. "Mother, there is naught I can say that will ever express what is in my heart. It overflows with love for you and I pray my wife shall be as you are, most wondrous and loving."

"As my heart overflows with love for you too." Tears

welled in her eyes and slipped free, tears she hadn't a chance of holding back.

Ivan moved toward his brother and gripped Kenneth's shoulder. "May you too find your mate and bear many cubs."

"Aye, as I wish the same for you." Kenneth clasped Ivan to him. They spoke to each other, in such a low tone she hadn't a chance of hearing it.

Ivan grinned, released Kenneth and strode to his destrier tethered to a post at the stables. He tightened his saddlebag into place and mounted his steed. With one last wave, he galloped through the fallen leaves lining the forest trail, his padded leather war coat donned and claymore holstered to his back. All too soon, he disappeared into the dark, taking a piece of her heart with him.

Kenneth wrapped his arms around her. "All will be well, Mother."

"Aye, it shall. Do you too sense your mate? I wish for a new daughter this night."

"She's very close, and I shall do all I can to give you what you seek." He motioned toward the village along the loch where the land curved to a tip. Smoke curled from several of the thatch-roofed houses high into the night sky. "I shall find her this night and bring her home."

"Then journey safely, and we shall see you on your return."

"You shall." He strode down to the sea-gate and bounded onto one of the moored skiffs.

Aye, this was a night of celebration. The coming days would mark the beginning of a new age, one filled with so many new promises for them all.

Chapter 3

A trickle of sunshine slithered between the gap in Iain's navy curtains where they hadn't quite been drawn and played over his closed eyelids. Curled in front of him, her back to his chest, Isla stirred and wriggled her pert backside into his groin. Holding and talking to her throughout the night had brought such peace to his soul.

Under his fur bedcovers, he ran one hand down her arm, her skin deliciously warm to the touch. For now he had this, her close, and it would be enough until they completed the bond.

"Iain?" Mumbling, she stretched and rolled toward him.

"Go back to sleep."

"Is it morning already?" She opened one eye and peered toward the window. "It is. Daniel will be calling soon." She sat up and the covers slithered down and pooled at her waist. "Would it be possible for me to take a shower before breakfast? And beg you for a change of clothes?"

"Of course, and no begging needed. I'll find my mother and ask her to secure what you'll need." He eased out of the bed, helped her to her feet and led her into his bathroom with its sandy-colored stone floor tiles, charcoal vanity and fluffy cream towels. "Any other requests?"

"Coffee. A big cup, black, no sugar. I'll need that if you want to get anything sensible out of me this morning."

"Clothes and coffee. You shower and I'll be back in fifteen minutes with both." He claimed a quick kiss, backed out of the bathroom and closed the door with a soft snick. He changed, donned a pair of black leather pants and a silver-threaded cotton t-shirt then laced his boots and sheathed his wrist dagger. At the door, he stopped, one hand on the brass knob as in his bathroom, the water drummed against the glass sides of the shower. Everything within him pricked at leaving her.

Except he had no choice.

Out the door, he walked and downstairs.

Within the great hall, a good hundred of his clansmen sat eating at trestle tables, their boisterous chatter relaxing him. His kin would be excited to hear his news, to know he'd found his chosen one. There was much to celebrate this day.

At the dais, his father sat dressed in a navy cotton-ribbed shirt over loose tan pants, his sword gleaming at his side in readiness for training after the morning meal. His mother sat next to him in a plum ankle-length skirt and blouse, and Finlay and Kirk joined them, their plates overflowing with bacon and eggs.

He weaved around the perimeter of the hall, pulled out the chair next to his father and grinned. "I have good news."

Dad grinned back at him as he stabbed a wedge of sausage and smeared it through the tomato sauce on the side of his plate. "Would that news have something to do with the young woman you steered inside the keep after sunset, the one you ferreted away in your chamber and didn't introduce to us all?"

"The very one."

Finlay leaned forward in his camouflage cargo pants and black shirt. "Then that explains the blast of contentment I got along our brotherly bond during the night. I returned from the chase of my mated one halfway through the night because I sensed your excitement. Congrats."

"Thanks. Her name is Isla."

Kirk clasped his shoulder. "I caught sight of your Isla when I was in the control room. I got the same blast of contentment that Finlay did. She's a pretty wee bear."

"She's also the eldest daughter of her clan's chief. Murdock Matheson. He's a seer, his mate having passed not long after Isla was born."

"That had to have been hard." Dad slid one arm around his mother's shoulders and drew her closer. "What skill does Isla hold?"

"She can compel and she's very strong. I couldn't move a muscle when she told me not to move."

"And why would she tell you not to move?" A teasing twinkle lit his father's eyes.

"We were setting boundaries at the time." Boundaries of a good sort. "She and her partner are working a case that brought her right to our doorstep. Capturing her last night, and just as the moon rose, was a stroke of good luck."

"Where's her partner now?" His mother stirred a teaspoon of honey into her cup of tea, her wavy hair, the same dark shade as his and his brothers' hair, swishing about her shoulders in a soft bob.

"His name is Daniel and the two were going to chat again this morning."

"You'll need to take great care if she holds the skill of compelling." Dad munched on his sausage. "Did you complete the bond?"

"We spent much of the night talking. Isla explained why she's run these past five years, and that she has no intention of losing her father. I've assured her she never will, although I've yet to learn the whereabouts of her home base."

"Give her time. She must first learn to trust you." Dad picked up a piece of buttered toast and bit into it. "Your mother and I will gladly reassure her she has her freedom, if that's what you wish for us to do."

"Of course she has her freedom." Mum reached across Dad's lap and squeezed Iain's arm. "You should also consider taking a week or two off, take her away and spend some time with her. Just the two of you. Unlike every other mated pair in our clan, you two haven't known each other your entire lives."

"As long as no one here minds that I do, I'm in total agreement." Being alone with Isla was exactly what he needed. "Mum, Isla arrived with nothing. Do you think you can rustle up a change of clothing for her?"

"I certainly can. What else might she need?"

"Breakfast, and a large cup of coffee, black, no sugar."

"Lovely." She rose and kissed his cheek. "That sounded like an invitation to go and introduce myself to her. I'll bring her down with me when I return."

Kirk poured a cup of steaming coffee from the flask in the center of the table and nudged it toward Iain. "If her father is the seer of her people, what's the likelihood we can talk to him about our missing mates, Finlay's and mine?"

"I've already mentioned your search to Isla and about how otherworldly it is. I'll bring it up again the moment I can." He'd do anything he could to aid his brothers in their pursuit of their chosen ones, just as they would do the same for him. "I need you two to keep an eye out for her partner. Daniel holds the ability of telekinesis and can lift a man with his mind along. I don't doubt he'll turn up here before too long. He and Isla are close, very close."

"Will do." Kirk rolled the cuffs of his dark shirt to the elbow, exposing the sheathed daggers at his wrists. "Did you have any issue with said partner last night?"

"He had his own problems to deal with. They were hunting two rogue bears from the offshoot clan of Mathies when I found her. The rogues got away and neither Daniel or Isla intend to give up the chase."

"There aren't many shifters left within the Mathie's diluted blood line," Kirk said. "Those who can shift can only do so on the night of a full moon."

"Iain!" Mum hurried toward him, her silk scarf a vivid streak of plum flapping behind her. "There's no sign of Isla in your chamber and the shower was left running."

He shoved back his chair and eyed his brothers. "Secure the keep. Lock everything down. She's not leaving here without me."

"I'm on it." Finlay raced out the door.

Kirk gritted his teeth. "I'll check with the guard in the control room. If she's left, we'll soon know it."

* * * *

Near the postern gate at the rear of Ivanson Castle, Isla compelled the guardsman on duty, her voice floating around him in its divine way. "You've never seen me and will have no knowledge I've walked this way. You'll even turn any surveillance footage off and rewind and tape over any images of me."

"Aye, miss." Cloudy eyed, he stepped aside and allowed her to pass.

With Iain's car key in hand, she snuck through the gate and raced across the gravel lot to his red convertible parked at the rear. Engine on, car in gear, she busted down the private winding road lined with thick pine trees either side. She hadn't wanted to leave Iain like this, but if she'd stayed a moment longer, Daniel would turn up and right now they had no time to lose. Finding the Mathies was too important to let it slide a moment longer.

Her cell phone rang and she dug it from her pocket and answered it. "Hey, Daniel."

"Hey back at ya. Where are you?"

"I'm coming. I'll be at the inn in five minutes." She pressed the button for the window and it lowered with a gentle hum. A cool breeze fluttered the short sleeves of Iain's black shirt, the very one he'd worn last night. She hadn't been able to leave without something of his that held his scent, and so before she'd slunk out of his room, she'd nabbed it and tied the two front flaps together over her own clothes.

Goodness. Her man smelled delectable, like woodsy pine and sunshine. She wanted to roll around in an open meadow with him, surrounded only by the beauty of the outdoors and kiss him again until he made her body hum like he had last night.

"Are you all right?" Daniel's question broke her happy reverie.

"Aye, Iain was the perfect gentleman, but he'll be on my six the second he realizes I've gone." Or she certainly hoped he would be. She wasn't yet ready to give up tangling with him until the next full moon rose.

"I've got the engine running. The chief scoured through satellite images taken of this area last night before it got too dark. He was able to confirm a match on the description I gave him of the Mathies' mustard-colored Jeep. They passed through the village thirty miles to the west, the same village we passed through on our way here. He's got evidence of them turning off the main road and crossing Milliner's Bridge. There's a large property on the right, one holding acres and acres of corn."

"Who owns the property?"

"A man by the name of Gerald Mathie-Bourner, ninety years of age, although he's recently deceased and the property is sitting in trust until the reading of the will. There's nothing on the property but an old and somewhat dilapidated shack. The chief's waiting for further satellite images to come through on the shack this morning. He's hoping the Jeep is still there."

"Who's Gerald Mathie-Bourner, and why hasn't that name cropped up until now?"

"The old man was a recluse who barely left his property. How close are you now?"

"Two minutes, no more." She squealed around the corner, flicking stones onto the grassy verge. "This time we'll find them and haul them in by their balls." She hung up, tossed her phone onto the leather seat next to her and drove like a wild woman.

Right on time, two minutes later, she skidded into the parking lot, dust pluming into the air. She wound the window up with an inch gap to spare at the top, grabbed her ringing phone that displayed an unknown number, locked the car and slid the key through the gap. It bounced on the tan leather seat and sprang onto the floor.

Sprinting, she raced to the SUV and slid into the front seat next to Daniel. "Go," she said then answered her phone, a whole lot out of breath, "Hello, you've reached Isla."

A low growl rumbled down the line. "Where the hell are you?"

"Clever bear. How'd you get my number?" Her mate was very resourceful.

"I memorized it before you hung up from Daniel yesterday. Now, would you care to answer my question? I'm missing my mate and I gave her my express promise she wouldn't leave my lair without me."

"Sorry, but I decided to take the convertible for a spin. She drives like a beauty, and now I'm back on the clock. I also borrowed your shirt. I really needed it. I hope you don't mind."

Daniel tore around the corner, pulled onto the main road and blew down the highway.

"What I mind is not knowing where you are."

"Don't worry about your baby. I left her locked in the parking lot at the inn. The key is inside."

"That's not the baby I'm after." One gloriously low drawl that made her ache in places she shouldn't be aching, or at least while on the clock. "Give me your destination. I'll follow you."

"I'm on clan business."

Daniel whizzed past a gas station. Ahead, past the rolling fields of lush grass, the stone steeple of a church rose high within a quaint village. Daniel tapped her leg. "Put Iain on speaker. Let me have a chat with him."

"Sure." She pressed the speaker button. "Iain, meet Daniel and play nice."

"I'd rather play nice with you." That deeply sexy voice of his was going to be her undoing.

"Iain"—Daniel cleared his throat—"I apologize for taking your mate from you so soon after you met her, except right now we're on the clock as she said and after two killers. Saving the life of innocents comes first. I hope you understand."

"I understand, but you still have no right to take her from me." A car engine roared to life, and then a door slammed shut, the dual sounds loud coming down the line.

"Follow us then," Daniel offered. "Since it sounds like you're on your way. We're headed to Milliner's Bridge, half an hour due west of here. There's a large property on the right. You know where I'm talking?"

"There's nothing but fields of corn in that area. Who owns the property you're speaking about?"

"An old man by the name of Gerald Mathie-Bourner owned the place. He's now deceased and the reading of his will is yet to be completed. We're going to park out of sight just off the road. The shack is a mile farther down the drive. Ensure you're well-armed." Daniel glanced at her. "My phone's in the glove compartment. The chief sent me a few satellite images of the turnoff and the bridge. Send them to your mate. I wouldn't want him to get lost."

"I won't get lost, but send the images to one of my brothers' cell phones." Iain's husky voice sent another delicious burst of heat curling through her.

"What are their numbers?" She fanned her flushed face.

Iain rattled them off.

She keyed both numbers in then added his as well when he recited it.

Daniel slowed as he drove through the village then sped up the moment they cleared the town's speed restriction.

"We just passed through the village, Iain. Where are you?"

"Close on your tail. The black SUV. We're catching up quick."

She gripped the side of her chair and looked through the rear darkened window. One of the large vehicles with enhanced tires that she'd seen in the castle's lot sped down the road in hot pursuit. "I hope you've got your seat belt on, Mr. Bear."

"I do."

She smiled and let her next words float to him, the truth within each and every one. "I miss you."

"Prove it." A deep rumbling purr.

"Oh, I intend to." She blew him a kiss even though he'd never see it.

"If you're getting all hot and bothered"—Daniel frowned—"then jump into the back and shift. There's plenty of room in there for your little bear."

"Smarty-pants." She cuffed him on the arm. "I'm not shifting in front of you. You've got your own little bear who likes to get naked and dance attendance on you." To Iain, she said, "Just ignore Daniel. He's got the worst sense of humor, but I promise you, you'll get used to it." She lowered her voice, whispered into the phone for Iain alone. "And I promise from now on, I'll only ever shift in front of you."

The SUV behind them swerved then moved back into its lane.

Daniel chuckled. "The man's already fallen under your spell." He turned off the main highway, crossed Milliner's Bridge and made another right into the driveway they were after. He bumped across the pot-holed entrance and snuck into a small flattened area in the front field of corn, their vehicle hidden within the towering rows surrounding them.

"Let's go and kick some bear ass." Daniel holstered his weapon and came around and opened her door.

She hung up her cell phone and jumped out as Iain rumbled in beside them. He flung open his door and marched toward her in thigh-hugging black leather pants and a silver cotton t-shirt, his holstered weapon peeking out from under his flapping leather jacket. Two men flanked him, both identical to Iain, the one on his right in camouflage cargo pants and a black shirt. He slung a military sniper's rifle over his shoulder. The man on his left wearing fawn pants and army boots, gripped a glinting gun.

"This is Finlay." Iain motioned to his right. "And on my left is Kirk." Leaving his brothers behind, he stopped in front of her, his fierce golden gaze boring in to hers. "You. Left. Me."

"I thought we already covered this." He stepped forward and she scrambled back and came up hard against the SUV. "I didn't have a—" He kissed her, one hand cupping the back of her head and the other seizing her hip as he dragged her against him.

She shouldn't allow him to push her around, only that thought flittered right out of her head under the searing heat of his mouth. Instead, she reached up on her toes, wound her arms around his neck and met him kiss for kiss. Now this kind of delicious kissing she could get used to.

"Excuse me." Daniel cleared his throat. "We've bad dudes to capture and all that."

Iain growled low in his throat as he lifted his head from hers and eyed Daniel. "In the future, where she goes, I go."

"Provided you don't keep her beyond our clan's reach, I'm good with that."

"No arguing, boys." She ducked under Iain's arm and extended her hand to Finlay and Kirk. "I didn't mean to be rude. Nice to meet you both."

"Welcome to the family." Finlay shook her hand then slid one thumb underneath his sniper rifle's front slung belt.

"The same welcome goes for me. It's nice to finally have a sister." Kirk hugged her then stepped back with a grin. "Very few people can catch my brother out the way you have today, and have for the past five years. I've been in awe of your talents for a while."

"Oh, ah, thank you." Barely hiding her smile, she gestured toward her partner. "This is Daniel, and please be very careful around him. He holds the skill of telekinesis and likes to pull all sorts of interesting stunts."

"I'd like to see your skill at work." Finlay shook Daniel's hand. "That's when we're not chasing two killers. Rogue bears, I've been told."

"They sure are. Owen and Ewan Mathie make up two of the four shifters we're aware of in their offshoot clan. On the night of the last full moon, they killed two innocent people and now they've tasted human blood, there's no knowing what they'll do next. We've been ordered to capture and contain." He eyed everyone in turn. "Since we all appear set to go, Finlay, you take the right, Kirk the left. The rest of us will span out through the center. Keep your senses alert. We're headed toward the shack a mile along the driveway through the corn."

Finlay trotted into the towering stalks on the right while Kirk disappeared into the field on the left. She jogged in after Daniel and Iain matched her step for step at her side. They ran the mile through the soft dirt, the corn stalks waving in the gentle breeze a good three feet above her head. Then when Daniel raised a hand they slowed and crouched at the periphery of the corn and all huddled next to him.

Two rows of corn remained between them and a wooden-boarded shack. The corn swept in a circle around a dusty front yard bare of even one single tree. In the center of the yard was a mustard-colored Jeep coated in dust, the same one from the inn and standing in front peering inside the raised hood was a middle-aged man in mechanic's overalls and a cap stuck backwards on his head. He planted one hand on the grill and whipped an oily rag hanging from his back pocket out and unscrewed a cap.

"That's neither of the Mathie brothers," she whispered, "although that Jeep is theirs."

"I'll take a pic." With his cell phone in hand, Daniel snapped an image of the mechanic with the shack in the background then sent it through to the chief.

Iain hunkered behind her, slid one arm around her waist and tucked her back into the V of his spread legs, his heat and fresh pine scent surrounding her. "Any idea who that is?" he murmured in her ear.

"No, but I'm going to find out." She kept her tone low but used her ability to compel to its greatest degree. "Iain, Finlay, and Kirk, you'll not utter a word in protest about my leaving, or try to restrain me, but you will all cover me." She winked at Daniel. "I need to get closer so only the mechanic can hear me. You get ready to check out the shack."

"Will do, and you're going to be in so much trouble with the big bear after this." Daniel grinned. "I can't wait to tell Emma about you and your mate. She's going to love hearing about what's gone down."

"She's going to hate she missed out on it too."

"She sure will." To the others, he said, "Keep an eye on the feisty one for me after I leave. She can be a handful at times. She also takes a bit of work to rope in."

"Be careful," Iain warned her, thankfully his words not a protest. No one had cracked her compelling yet, but if anyone could, it might very well be him.

"I will." She kissed his cheek. "You'll learn to trust my abilities soon enough then I won't need to compel you at all." She slipped out of his grasp and crawled one row closer so she couldn't be seen but could still easily project her voice.

Iain crawled in over top of her, shielding her completely with his body then flattened her to the ground. "Just covering you, as requested. Two can play at your game, little bear."

"I might be little, but I have sharp claws. Lift up a touch." He did and she smirked. "There's no taming a compeller."

On one side of them, Kirk moved into position and on the other, Finlay eased lower onto his belly, his sniper's rifle propped on top of the dirt and his eye to the sight.

Daniel swept out a few rows, moving closer toward the shack then gave her a nod. They worked well in tandem and he'd wait for her okay to go in.

"We're ready." Iain trained his weapon on the mechanic.

"Mechanic man, here my voice and don't acknowledge it. Nothing is out of the ordinary, but you're going to wander closer toward me in the corn field then act as if your boot lace is untied. I want you to kneel and tie it back up. Don't draw any unnecessary attention to yourself while you do so."

The man swaggered their way, a peek of scraggly brown hair showing from under his cap. He lowered to one knee and grasped his boot lace.

"Who's with you, and why are you here?" she demanded. "Answer me in a quiet voice."

"No one's with me, and I'm fixing my cousin's Jeep."

"Who's your cousin?"

"Owen Mathie."

"Whose place is this? Give me as much information as you can."

"Grandpa Mathie-Bourner's, but he passed away over a month ago. No one lives here anymore. We need to sell the place, just waiting on the lawyers, the will being read and all."

"Where are Owen and Ewan?"

"They took off for the bunker in my truck. Said they'd leave the truck somewhere for me to pick up once they were done with it. They'll call. They always do when they need a hand."

Iain growled in her ear. "The Mathies are cunning."

"And now they know we're chasing them." She lifted a hand toward Daniel. "You catch all that?"

"Sure did. I'll go check out the shack."

"Be careful." She returned her gaze to the mechanic. "Mechanic man, I want you to keep your focus on my voice. You won't see anyone moving about. What's your name and where's the bunker?"

"Name's Gerry Mathie-Bourner, and I'm named after my gramps. No idea where the bunker is. My cousins are into some weird stuff that I've got nothing to do with it, but they're kin, so I've gotta help where I can."

"Can you shift?"

"Nah, only the two of them and their sisters can, and only on the night of the full moon. Rest of the time their ability to shift won't rise. Blood's too weak." A confirmation of what they'd already known. He snorted then frowned as he worked his boot lace. "Stupid thing won't do up right."

Daniel snuck out of the corn field, crept onto the verandah then opened the creaky front door and whipped inside. Three magpies soared in a circle overhead.

"Gerry, give me your address and your phone number."

He spoke it and she wriggled her cell phone from her pocket and sent the information to Daniel and Dad. "Gerry, how often do your cousins come out here?"

"Three or four times a year, just when they're swinging by."

"When they call you, I want you to call the number I give you and tell the man you speak to all the details your cousins pass on to you. You'll remember this number with ease when it's needed, although you won't remember why you must do as I've asked, nor shall you remember speaking to me or anyone else about this." She recited the chief's direct cell phone number.

"Right. I can do that."

"Very good, Gerry."

Daniel snuck out of the shack and dove back into the corn field. He shuffled toward her and said, "It's all clear in there. Two tiny back rooms along with a kitchen and living area, although there's nothing but dust coating moth-eaten furniture. The electricity's on but nothing's running off it. I got your cell phone message."

"Gerry's going to call the chief when his cousins get in touch with him."

"Good job. Send the mechanic on his way."

"Gerry, go back to what you were doing. You're all alone at your grandpa's shack."

Gerry stood, rubbed the dirt from his knee and strode back to the Jeep.

Iain scooped her off the ground, set her on her feet and steered her back the way they'd come, his brothers and Daniel walking along the corn rows either side of them. All kept a watchful eye on their surroundings.

"I've got a call coming in." Daniel holstered his weapon and answered it on speaker. "Hey, Chief. Isla and I picked up an additional team of men. Iain and his brothers, Finlay and Kirk."

"I just had a vision of them. I'm not surprised about the addition to your team. I've got Nathan checking into this so-called bunker, and I'm running a check on Gerry's truck."

"Dad." She edged closer to Daniel so her father could hear her. "Gerry said his cousins visit him three or four times a year, just when they're swinging by. He's got your number and I requested he call you if they visit. I added the usual demands, no recall and all."

"Good work, although since we're now stuck in a waiting game, there's nothing more any of us can do until we catch a break somewhere or the Mathies surface again." He cleared his throat. "If you wish, spend some time with Iain then return when you're ready. In the meantime, Daniel can team up with Nathan."

"Are you sure?" She'd love the time off to get to know her mate, but if her father needed her, she'd return.

"I'm positive, honey."

"Who's going to keep you on your toes while I'm gone?"
She strode through the weedy dirt, the prophecy on her mind.
*Gilleoin's sons will separate when they come of age and rule
their own clans, yet there will come a time far in the future when
a mated bond forms between the two clans. Only then must
Gilleoin's descendants once again merge, and the 'power of
three' be unveiled.* Aye, a mated bond had formed and it was
time to embrace her changing future.

"You're never far from me, Isla, no matter the distance
separating us."

"Then I'll call you tomorrow, let you know how things are
going."

Daniel lifted the phone closer to his mouth. "Chief, I'd like
to meet Isla's new kinfolk before I head back. I'll drive to
Ivanson Castle first then return. I should be back by nightfall."

"Travel safely." Dad didn't question Daniel's need and
neither did she. Both of them always had her back.

Daniel hung up while beside her, Iain walked with purpose.

Finlay cast her a look. "It must be interesting having a seer
in the family."

"It's both interesting and frustrating. One can get into a
whole lot of trouble, and that's without even stepping one foot
out of line. Dad has visions of things that can happen well before
their time."

"That's unfair for you." Kirk chuckled, a cheeky look on
his face. "My parents would have loved to have had forewarning
of all the mayhem we got up to as kids."

"It's just as well they didn't." Iain moved ahead and lifted
some fallen stalks barring her way.

She ducked under his arm, her gaze on his as she skipped
backward. "What kind of mayhem did you three cause? Spill
some dirt."

"Since I'm already aware of all the dirt, I'll scout ahead and
make sure everything's clear." Kirk nodded at Iain and
disappeared.

"There's no one around. I can't scent anyone, can you?"
She pressed one hand against Iain's chest and stopped him in his
tracks. Standing in front of him, she tipped her head to the side.
"Come on. Share some of the good stuff with me."

Daniel and Finlay kept walking and she waited, holding her place, not giving in.

Iain narrowed his gaze, those golden eyes of his focused fully on her. "There's a lifetime of good stuff to share, and I intend to tell you every juicy detail of our shenanigans, but not right now." He glanced over her head, his gaze drilling into Daniel's back. "You two are closer than I'd imagined and it raises the hairs on my neck."

"Daniel is devoted to Emma and their baby boy."

"Yet you and he are partners."

"We grew up together and our skills, once combined, work seamlessly as one." She stroked his chest through his shirt. "I realize our relationship as partners is tighter than most, but we've been through so much together. Daniel's the closest I'll ever get to having an overbearing older brother."

"I like that you said 'overbearing' and 'brother.'" He covered her hand with his, twined their fingers together. "I'll be less on edge once we've completed our bond. I apologize now for any difficult moments ahead. I'm sure there will be many."

"I'll forgive you, provided you give me one juicy detail, enough to keep me happy."

"There was this one time"—he kissed the tip of her nose— "when the three of us decided it was time to up the ante on our sword training. We all swapped out our childhood wooden swords for the real deal, and after we did, we snuck outside in the dark of the night and battled each other in the training yard."

"Did any of you get hurt?"

"We could barely raise those massive steel swords. We must have been all but six at the time." A smile lit his eyes. "I almost cut my toe off when I dropped the blade and Finlay stuck the end of his into Kirk's butt when he tried to swing it. Kirk couldn't sit for a week and Finlay and I couldn't stop laughing."

"That's priceless." She chuckled, imagining all he'd said. "Do you still train together?"

"Our clan adheres to the old ways. We train daily just in order to expend our excess energy."

"So do all within my clan." She rubbed her cheek against his chest, drawing his scent to her skin. As she did, he straightened the collar of her shirt, his fingers sliding over her nape and tangling in her hair.

In her ear, he whispered, so sensually, "I intend for us to build a lifetime of memories together, ones we'll cherish forever. Would you like that?'

"It sounds divine."

"Then we'll begin by indulging in an escape, one you'll require some essentials for."

"Essentials? You mean like clothing and such?"

"Aye, that's exactly what I mean." Holding her hand, he led her back along the track and into the small clearing where they'd parked. He opened the rear door of his SUV and she hopped inside and shuffled along while he called out to Daniel, "Pull over at the village's department store on your way through. My mate's riding with me."

"Sure thing." Daniel drove out first.

Kirk took the wheel and Finlay sat beside him while Iain buckled her in and spread his arm along the top of the backseat. He played with her hair, his fingers sliding through her long locks as they crossed the bridge and turned onto the main road. She lowered her window and sighed as the fresh country breeze chased across her heated flesh. His touch warmed her as nothing else could.

Leaning closer, he nipped her ear. "No more running. I want your agreement on that."

"No more running." She looked into his eyes, the promise of her words in her own. "Right now, I want some time alone with you, as promised. Although I won't allow the Mathies to get away and neither will Daniel. That case takes precedence over all else."

"I agree. The innocent must be protected but from now on, we'll work the same cases, whether that's alongside Daniel and your kin, or with my brothers and my clan. I won't take you away from your family, but so too I won't leave my own."

"One of my greatest fears in finding you has always been what I might lose in the process." She rested her cheek against his shoulder. "I need my father and he needs me."

"You won't lose him. I'll make sure of it."

Her mind stretched and battered against his, trying to force its way in. A pathway would remain elusive until they'd completed the bond. She squeezed her eyes shut, the pressure intensifying tenfold.

"Are you all right?" He rubbed one thumb over her scrunched forehead.

"My mind demands the link too, just as yours did last night."

"Then we'll need to do something about it. I found touch helps." He caught her hand, brought her palm to his lips and kissed her. He was right. A little of the pressure eased in her mind from his touch, although she needed far more touch than what he'd so far offered.

She claimed his mouth and he opened his lips under hers and kissed her in return, a heady merging of mouths that left her breathless and dizzy for more.

More she couldn't also wait to claim.

Regardless of her running, her mate was all she'd ever secretly hoped he'd be.

Chapter 4

The ancient House of Clan Matheson, 1210.

Kenneth's course was set. He strode along the stone sea-gate landing, released his skiff's mooring rope, coiled and stored it under the center seat and with the oars in hand, rowed beyond the breakers. As the wind picked up, he tucked the oars away, seized the ropes and raised the sail. The wind filled it with a hearty slap and with his feet braced wide along the side, he steered his boat as it shot off like an arrow.

Along the loch, the village lay and the lass who would soon be his. All his senses honed in on her. Hell, all of his life, he'd known she would be close and a week past when he'd visited the village to aid his mother and grandmother's fae people in the search for a lost child, he'd been entranced by Elizabeth, the elder sister of the lost lad. 'Twas as if his soul had already recognized their mated bond. Her anguish had gripped him and wouldn't let go.

That night, he'd shifted form with his father and searched the woods, tracking the lad by his scent alone and when they'd found him huddled deep within the dense brush on the cold and damp ground, a little of his anguish had eased. Elizabeth's brother, although suffering a broken leg, would survive that day.

The wind plastered his tunic against his chest and whipped his shoulder-length hair about his neck as he sailed toward the sleepy village. Houses of stone and clay, cloistered tightly together and surrounded by a high stone wall, beckoned him with the promise of the one who awaited him within.

He steered his skiff toward land, lowered the sail as he neared the pebbly shore and jumped into the knee-deep water. He hauled his boat half onto the beach then stopped as the faint fragrance of lavender and all things sweet reached him. 'Twas Elizabeth's scent, one that had embedded itself deep into his mind the week before.

"Kenneth!" Elizabeth raced through the gap in the stone perimeter wall, her blue gown swishing about her legs and her long golden-blond locks catching the moonlight and shining like silk as her hair streamed behind her. She hurried down the stony trail, onto the beach and bounded into his arms. He barely planted one foot back in time to cease them both from toppling over. "I knew you'd come for me this eve," she breathed in a rush. "Your grandmother spoke to me after you found my brother. She said I would be the one and to remain in wait for you."

His grandmother was a sneaky one.

Filled with joy, he twirled Elizabeth around then set her back on her feet and lowered to one knee. Holding her hand in his, he spoke the words drawn from deep within his soul. "You're my mate, the one woman I wish to share my life with. Will you do me the great honor of becoming my wife?"

"Aye, I'd like that very much." Her eyes sparkled, such a striking hue of sapphire. "Would you like to speak to my father?"

"Nay, I shall simply steal you away and inform him on the morrow that you're to be my bride." He swung her into his arms, leaned over the side of his skiff and set her gently on the center seat then pushed the boat into the water and leapt aboard.

Tonight was their night, and no other's. He would woo his chosen one as she deserved and she would be his, for all time. Exhilaration, unlike any he'd ever known before, surged through him.

Chapter 5

Panting for breath in the back seat of the SUV, Iain nipped Isla's lower lip then pulled back an inch as Kirk drove them toward the village. His woman could distract him completely with her passionate, mind-bending kisses.

"Where are you going?" She tugged him back and nuzzled his neck, her teeth razzing over his skin. If she bit him now, he'd be hard-pressed to hold back. If only they were alone.

Kirk pulled into a parking space on the main street next to Daniel's vehicle.

The department store in front with its wide glass doors set within a sandstone brick frontage sat between a three-story tavern with accommodations on the top two levels and a florist shop with a bright red door and hanging baskets of colorful flowers.

"This village looks so quaint."

"My mother adores this department store. She insists it sells everything one could ever need. You should be able to find all you're after here." He hopped out, came around the back and opened her door. He led her up onto the pavement then gently wiped a streak of dry dirt from her cheek.

"Maybe we could grab a bite to eat afterward. I missed breakfast." She glanced at the tavern next door to the store. "Do we have time for that?"

"We'll make time." He clapped Kirk on the shoulder as he joined them. "Reserve us a table. Order for me if you like."

"Will do." Kirk wandered into the tavern that held a restaurant they patronized regularly.

Isla rounded the hood of Daniel's car, opened the passenger door and nabbed a red leather purse from the front seat.

Finlay stepped in beside him. "I'm glad you've got her back. Now, make sure you don't lose her again."

"Thanks for keeping me sane while we searched for her."

"No problem." Finlay followed in Kirk's footsteps.

Isla spoke to Daniel and the two hugged before her partner trailed after his brothers.

She sashayed across to him, caught his hand and tugged him inside the store. He pulled a trolley from the bay and weaved through the aisles as she browsed, her hips swaying far too enticingly in that super snug denim. All he wanted to do was drag her against him, stamp his mark on her as he had last night and ensure she never left his side again. The chase this morning to catch her had worn at his nerves. Hell, he really needed to be alone with her, and soon. He'd take her to the cabin. It was the perfect place.

In front of him, Isla thumbed through a rack of jackets, her golden gaze darting between the clothing and him. "Are you all right?"

"I'll be fine once I've got you alone."

"We're fairly alone now, give or take the odd shopper." She sidled closer, pressed her entire body against his, every glorious and curvy inch of her. "We could even call this our second date."

"If this is our second date, then I'm sorry about the tagalongs."

"I can handle them, plus I'm used to being around my clan and I'm rarely alone." She wandered from his side toward a carousel of jeans. She pulled a few pairs off it then rummaged through a pile of shirts on the shelves and slung her selection into the trolley. She added a swimsuit and shorts, skirts and blouses and a low-cut slinky red dress he couldn't wait to see her in. In the footwear department, she added Nike sneakers and socks, sandals, and a pair of sexy red five-inch heels that made his mouth water. "Time for undergarments." She winked. "This way, my big bear."

In the lingerie section he most definitely drooled as she flicked through lacy bras and skimpy thongs. She chose what she needed in her size then added a sheer white satin camisole and a pink nightie with bear paw prints on it. He palmed the print that matched his hand size to perfection. "I can't wait to see you in that, or out of it."

"Should I get the matching bed-socks, or do you want the honor of warming my toes at night?" She pressed him back into a gap between two racks of dressing gowns and on her tiptoes, kissed his chin. "By the way, you are bringing the naughty streak out in me. I'm usually such a good girl. I've never fraternized with a man in a department store before."

"I should hope you haven't, and I'll warm a lot more than your toes the moment you give me the word to."

"Sexy second date talk. I like it." She stepped back and walked across to the health and beauty section. After browsing, she selected some makeup, a toothbrush, and a packet of cosmetic wipes. She added her bundle to the growing pile then picked up a box of condoms and tapped the box. "Do we need these?"

The condoms stared him hard in the eye. His cock, already partially hard at being this near her, hardened to the point of pain. He cleared his dry throat. "That's entirely your choice. I'm happy with or without, although to complete the bond, we'll need to be skin on skin the first time."

She eyed the box and frowned. "Hmm."

"Tell me what you're thinking." He slid a finger under her chin and lifted her gaze to his.

"Clan births are down. It took Emma five years to fall pregnant and there was nothing medically preventing her from conceiving. Hers and Daniel's baby is the first cub to grace our clan in five years."

"It's been five years since our last clan birth too. Couples are struggling to conceive at Ivanson Castle and without any medical reason why."

"Do you think it's got something to do with the prophecy?"

"I don't know. Do you?"

"I've no idea. Something certainly isn't right though." She turned the box over. "So, the question is, do we use these or allow the natural course of events to unwind?"

"Whether we choose to use them or not is one decision we don't have to make right at this moment." He slid the box from her hands and added it to the trolley. "If you wish to use them, we shall. If not, then we'll discard them. Either way, my desire to be with you will never waver, condoms or not."

"Thank you." She peeked in both directions of the deserted aisle. "Can I tell you something rather personal?"

"Of course. You can speak to me about anything."

"I'm feeling hot just at the thought of completing the bond. I want your body sliding against mine, all skin on skin and nothing else. I'm also surprised by how much I want it. It's as if from the moment we met, the relationship I've denied us both these past five years is the one thing I want, and right now." She rubbed her chest against his and her hard nipples poked into him. "I want to touch you, for you to touch me. The desire is riding me hard."

"I feel the same way, and honestly, I'm about to come in my pants just from being this near you."

"Really?" She nibbled on her lower lip, her gaze skimming down to his crotch. "Would it be possible for me to touch you? I want to make you come like you did with me last night. It felt so good."

"Damn it, woman." There wasn't a chance he'd ever deny her such a request. All of him was hers. He pushed their trolley into an empty changing room at the end of the aisle, swept her inside with him then closed the door on their large cubicle. Stalking her, he caged her against the wall and planted both hands either side of her head. "Touch me as you please, but wherever you touch me, I'll touch you in return."

She wriggled the hem of his silver-threaded shirt up, her eyes widening on the bulge in his pants then gently, she caressed his cock and balls through the soft leather and smiled at him. "Do you like this kind of touch?"

"Immensely." And the word 'immensely' could barely express just how much, but his actions might. He captured her mouth with his and kissed her. He twined his tongue around hers and moaned as she rubbed him harder below. Turnabout was fair play. He opened her shirt—his shirt she'd tied together with the front flaps—and cupped her breasts through her tank top. Her nipples, so hard and pointy, demanded his touch. He pinched the tips then moaned as she opened the button-fly of his pants, freed his shaft and curled her fingers around him. One stroke was all it took for his balls to tighten and lift and when she swirled her thumb over his head, he shot his load into her hand. He grunted, the sound muffled against her neck as he bent over her. "Damn it. I didn't mean to come that fast. My apologies."

"Don't be sorry, because I intend to make you come again."

She continued to stroke him, and he got even harder. Surely coming twice in so short a time was impossible.

"I can see you're going to make me lose my mind, but I'm not losing it again without you." He opened her jeans, slid his hand inside her silk panties and rubbed her tight nub. Taking her mouth in a hot kiss, he devoured her until the sweet honey scent of her arousal rose and saturated his senses. When she gasped and shuddered in his arms, he slid one finger deep inside her channel and growled at the delicious tug of her inner muscles tightening on him, pulsing and pulling.

"Want you bad—need to bite you—still coming," she panted as her body squeezed him even harder.

If she wanted him, he'd give her exactly what she asked for. He gripped his jacket collar and shirt with his free hand and hauled it to the side of his neck, her orgasm still dragging his finger deep within her. "Bite me," he urged. "Now."

"Aye, my big bear." Still caressing his shaft, she sucked his offered skin and bit down, so hard he came, soaring over the edge of no return as she bucked against him, her channel sucking on his finger so greedily.

He held her as they both came back down, his heart beating a rapid tattoo against hers. "Isla," he murmured, "I can't wait to join with you fully."

"I can't wait to join with you either. My bear wants to play, and she intends to have her wicked way." Her knees wobbled and she clung to his shoulders. "Don't let me go. My limbs are like jelly."

"Tonight, we roam, just the two of us." He kissed her again, soft and languidly, then he forced himself to pull away before he took her all over again. When he joined with her fully, it'd be in complete privacy and in one of his favorite places on Earth.

"I tossed some cosmetic wipes in the trolley before. We could use them to clean up."

"Good thinking." He lifted the tab on the packet, pulled a bunch out and carefully wiped her hand of his come then himself and buttoned his pants.

She tended to herself below, straightened her clothing and binned the cloths in the corner trash can where he'd tossed his. "Now I'm really hungry." One sexy smile.

"Then allow me to feed my little bear."

* * * *

After leaving the checkout area, Isla walked outside to the SUV as Iain carried her purchases. Mmm, her core still tingled from the exquisite orgasms he'd given her, one that had toppled right over the next as he'd made her soar from her body and reach the stars.

He opened the trunk and as he set her bags inside, she leaned against his back and stroked his broad shoulders. She caressed downward, over his rigid biceps and back up again. "I hope you don't mind public displays of affection."

"I'd be a fool if I did." He closed the trunk and faced her, his eyes a molten pool of liquid gold. "My body is yours to touch, as and when you wish."

"The same goes for you."

"Then that will make for an interesting time away together." He twined their fingers and led her though the tavern's front door and past a corner table in the entranceway with a decorative oak-aged beer barrel with the Innis and Gunn stamp emblazoned on the front.

A long carpet runner of rich burgundy and blue ran the length of the wooden floor in front of the bar up ahead. Standing behind the bar's polished oak countertop was a portly barman dressed in black pants and a white shirt with a red and blue checked tea towel slung over one shoulder. He poured a drink for a business man dressed in a gray suit who perched on one of the four barstools.

Behind the bar stood a tall display cabinet with engraved wooden columns and intricately designed architraves, its shelves filled with beer mugs, shot glasses and wine and champagne flutes. This tavern looked so similar to the one at home where she and Dad ate every Sunday. They usually ordered her mother's favorite meal, bangers and mash. She'd miss this Sunday's meal, only two days away. A wave of sadness washed through her.

"You've gone quiet all of a sudden." Iain stroked the inside of her palm with his thumb as they wandered across the room toward Daniel and his brothers seated at a large round table, their legs kicked out in front of them and beer mugs in hand.

"I'm reminiscing. Every Sunday Dad and I eat out at the local pub. There aren't many Sundays we miss. Only those when work calls us away. Dad started the tradition with Mum before she passed."

"How did that happen, her passing? If you don't mind me asking?"

"You can ask me anything you like, and she had cancer. She discovered a lump in her breast during the early stages of her pregnancy with me. They operated but she wouldn't allow the doctors to treat her any further than that, not while she was expecting. Unfortunately, the cancer spread quickly. She was so sick toward the end and the doctor delivered me as soon as he could. She passed just a week after I was born." Tears welled in her eyes. "She gave up her life so I could have mine."

"She loved you, right from the very beginning." He cupped her cheek, stroked his fingers back and forth.

"That's why I can't lose my father. His heart was broken when she passed and all he wished for was to join her in her death. He would have taken his own life if not for me and the fact my mother had made him promise to give me all the love he held inside him, to raise me as she would have." She snuggled deeper into his touch.

"You'll never lose him, and of that I give you my absolute word."

"Thank you." She'd hold onto his word, knew to the depths of her soul he spoke the truth.

He led her around the table and pulled out a chair for her next to Daniel.

"You're crying." Daniel eyed her then scowled at Iain. "Do I need to hurt someone?"

"I was telling Iain about my mother and how she passed."

"Ah, I see." Daniel tucked a lock of her hair behind her ear, as affectionate with her as he always was. Growing up together, tussling as young cubs and later in life, relying on each other as partners, had forged a bond between them no one could break.

"Hands off my woman." Iain leaned forward, his gaze as hard as shards of ice on Daniel.

"No, no, no." She gripped Iain's leather-clad thigh and rubbed. "You two aren't allowed to fight because of me. There's no taming an alpha male's bear, but I'm certainly going to try."

"Here's our waitress," Daniel intervened.

Fabulous. Perfect timing. She smiled at the blond-haired woman in her impeccably pressed black pants and tartan-collared white shirt as she set a platter of breads and dips on the table. The woman dipped her head then weaved back around the tables and through the swing door into the kitchen.

Daniel nudged a glass of lemon and lime bitters toward her. "I ordered this for you earlier, and a medium steak and salad along with a side order of fries."

"Extra ketchup?"

"Of course."

"Wonderful. Thanks." She swirled the ice around the frosty glass with the red straw then sipped her drink as Iain frowned at it. She eyed her beverage. "Is there something wrong with my drink?"

"He knows what to order you." He took a swig from his beer.

"Oh." Territorial bear. "Your brothers know what to order you, right?"

"They're my brothers."

"Same goes for Daniel. He's my brother, but I'll tell you what, you can ask me any question you like and I'll answer it. You have free reign. Go for it."

"Tell me your first childhood memory." He leaned forward, elbows on the table, interest gleaming in his eyes.

"Ah, except for that one. Next question."

"You said free reign, and I don't care for any secrets between us."

"Or between us as well." Finlay smeared a slice of warm crusty bread with garlic butter then leaned back in his chair. "As brothers, we're closer than most. It's essential we get to know you as well as Daniel clearly does."

"You are all so frustrating." It appeared she wouldn't get out of this one. After blowing out a long breath, she nodded. "All right, my first childhood memory involves nudity. Mine and Daniel's."

"Damn it." Iain gritted his teeth and snarled. "I should just lop off his head right now."

"You could have lied, little sister." Daniel chewed a slice of bread, every muscle tense as he kept one eye on Iain. "If I return to Emma missing a crucial appendage, you'll have her to answer to."

"Give me the details." Iain drummed his fingers on the burgundy placemat in front of him.

"I was four at the time. Dad took me down to the stream for a swim and Daniel was there with his mother. I had this frilly pink two-piece swimsuit on, one Dad had bought me for Christmas, but Daniel wasn't wearing a stitch of clothing. He was frolicking in the nude and loving it." She selected two slices of crusty bread and smeared them with cranberry feta and passed one to Iain. "So I ditched my swimsuit too not realizing boys looked quite different to girls until I got closer to Daniel in the water. Even at four, that appendage of his was rather impressive. Emma would definitely be furious if he lost it."

Daniel choked on his bread. "No more," he rasped. "Ask him what his earliest childhood memory is. You need to switch the subject now."

"Hold on." Iain hauled her chair smack up against his. "Do you recall this same memory?" he gritted at Daniel.

"I'm not the one who agreed to answer any questions."

"Answer me."

"Sheesh. All right. I'm a month older than Isla, and I'll never forget swimming in the stream with her. Her brown hair swung down to her waist, covering every part of her. I saw nothing, noth-ing." He swiped a hand in a definitive-no gesture across his neck. "That's my story and I'm sticking to it."

"I have your meals." The waitress beamed as she placed hers and Daniel's dishes before them, walked back to the kitchen and returned with Iain and his brothers' meals. "Is there anything else you'd all like?"

"I need a sharper knife," Iain demanded. "Pronto, please."

"No, he's fine." Isla smiled at the young woman. "Thanks for these meals."

"You're welcome." She strode over to the corner table where a family of four seated themselves and pulled out her notepad and pen from a pouch belted around her waist.

"You need to calm down." She picked up Iain's cutlery and

passed it to him. "Those pork chops of yours look delicious. They're a definite favorite of mine too. In fact, I'll eat any red meat provided it's tender and juicy. I like my chicken crumbed or in a sauce, and my fish as fresh as possible and pan-fried. All vegetables are a go, except tomatoes and cucumber. And I adore dessert, particularly if there's chocolate in the mix, then I'm all over it. Did you get all that? I'll repeat if needed."

"No, I heard every word, and you have my most grateful thanks for the information." He cupped her nape, brought her mouth to his and devoured her in a hungry kiss. When he let her go, she almost clambered onto his lap for more.

"Well, for that steamy kiss, I'll give you a promise. From this moment on, I'll never swim in the nude with any man other than you."

"I accept your promise and will hold you to it."

Perfect. One mate calmed, and one promise she was happy to uphold.

"Now, it's your turn, Iain. What's your first childhood memory?"

"Accepting the very first of Kirk's stupid dares. We were terrors when we were younger, always getting into trouble." He cut into his roasted potato drizzled in gravy and ate a forkful. "Around the age of four, Kirk challenged Finlay and me to climb the highest tree, the one that butted right up against the rear curtain wall."

"And did you climb it?"

"Kirk's always egging Finlay and me on to do stupid things, and being that Kirk's the youngest, we have a habit of giving into him. Can't let him get into trouble all on his own."

"I would have loved to have had a sibling, someone to share getting into trouble with." She cut into her steak.

Finlay popped a fry between his lips. Of the three of them, he had more freckles smattered across his nose and cheeks, as well as a rather beautiful Celtic tattoo on his right bicep. Kirk meanwhile had the same golden eyes as his brothers, but a glimmer of starburst yellow rimmed the edge. All three were the same in looks yet with the odd unique difference. Iain though, she'd never mistake him for his brothers. Just looking at him made her heartbeat pound and her body heat.

With his gorgeous gaze on her, Iain snuck one of her fries. "Are there any other seers in your clan, other than your father?"

"There's usually one born in every generation. They're particularly strong in my direct line, but Dad's the only one at the moment. We're overdue for a seer birth."

"I'd like to meet your father, as soon as it's possible."

"I'm sure he'd like to meet you too." Beside her, Daniel polished off his steak and rubbed his belly. He was being far quieter than usual. "Are you all right?" she asked him.

"The less I talk, the less trouble I get into."

"I see, although you'll still be in trouble if you didn't order me a dessert."

"I'd never forget that. I ordered *Death by Chocolate*."

"Oooh, yum. I love y—"

"No." He shoved a hand over her mouth. "Don't you dare speak words of love to me." He raised a brow. "Can I safely remove my hand?"

She pried his fingers away, one by one. "Sorry, clearly I'll need to learn to watch what I say in the future."

"Thank you." He motioned toward Iain. "Give him a calm-me-down kiss. That'd be helpful."

She turned to Iain. "I'm sorry, but I really love chocolate."

"You're not the one who needs to apologize." Fists clenched at his sides, his breath whistled out between tight lips. "You warned me your relationship with Daniel was tight. I don't mean to overreact. Just give me some more time to come to grips with the closeness of your bond."

"Truly?"

"Aye, truly, although a calm-me-down kiss wouldn't go a—"

"Excuse me." The waitress had returned, a smile on her face as she took the cleared plates away and another waitress set desserts before them all.

Isla swiveled her plate around to further appreciate the slice of gooey chocolate cake, a mound of hot fudge ice cream and wedges of dark and milk chocolate protruding from a swirl of rich chocolate mousse.

Across from her, Finlay spooned apple shortcake into his mouth and Kirk licked his lips as he eyed his apricot crumble drizzled with cream. Daniel thanked the waitress for his strawberry cheesecake and Iain stirred sugar into a cup of strong black coffee, no dessert in sight.

"Do you not like a sweet treat after a meal?" She plucked a wedge of milk chocolate from the mousse and ate it.

"I rarely eat anything sweet."

"Wow. That's almost a crime." She scooped ice cream into her mouth and sighed as the decadent confection slid over her tongue and sent her taste-buds dancing. "You have to try this." She offered him a spoonful and when he opened his mouth, she slipped it inside then waited until he'd swallowed. "It's good right?"

"It's very sweet." He leaned in, his mouth a whisper from hers. "But I'd rather taste it directly from your lips."

"I don't like sharing my chocolate. You're lucky you got the spoonful you did."

"Is that right?" His eyes gleamed with mischief, all sign of his frustration slipping away.

"That wasn't a dare."

"Sounded like it to me, my little bear."

* * * *

Iain sipped his coffee, his gaze on his woman. He'd missed out on five precious years with her and everything within him demanded he make back some of that time, however he could. Definitely time for an escape. From the moment they left this tavern, it'd be just the two of them. He'd ensure it.

Meals finished, he walked outside and held the front passenger door open for her. She slid inside, buckled up and while she did, he joined his brothers and Daniel on the pavement. "I'm taking her out to the cabin."

"A good idea." Finlay squeezed his shoulder. "Kirk and I'll ride with Daniel back to the inn. We'll pick your car up for you and take it back."

"I'd appreciate that. Isla left it locked up with the key inside, although I have a spare one on me." He removed the key from his chain and passed it to Finlay.

"Take as much time as you need. We'll see you when you return." Finlay jumped into the rear of Daniel's SUV while Kirk took the front seat beside Daniel.

"Where are they going?" Isla asked him as he eased in behind the wheel and started the engine.

"It's time for that escape I promised you. They're going to pick up my car and take Daniel for a tour of Ivanson Castle. They'll look after him before he heads back."

"So, where are we headed?" She lowered the window and the fresh breeze ruffled her silky long locks, the same exact shade of the rich chocolate mousse she'd enjoyed.

"Somewhere very special." He drove out of the village and along the winding highway edged on one side by the forest and on the other the rolling moors. "It'll be just the two of us for a while."

"And what makes this place so very special?" She rested her hand on his upper thigh, her fingers curled snugly around his leg.

"Five years ago, my brothers and I built a cabin deep in the woods on Matheson land. It's a retreat of sorts. We thrive being amongst our clansmen, but sometimes it's necessary for us to be alone, to strengthen our bonds as brothers." He covered her hand with his. "We fish in the stream, allow our bears to roam, that sort of thing."

"I'm so glad you have them."

"We're tight and always have each other's backs, just as they'll now have yours." He slid his fingers between hers. "Going forward, we'll live our life together, and when you need to return home to your father, then that's where we'll go." He turned off the main road, the one just before the inn, then bumped along a private driveway winding deep into Matheson territory. Pine, ash and elm trees rose high either side of the thin track. Ten miles in, he slowed then entered a clearing. His log cabin, with its two chimneys and wide wraparound porch painted a deep rustic-brown, had taken him and his brothers almost a year to build in between assignments. He pulled up in front and opened Isla's door.

"This place is amazing." She twirled around, her gaze bright as she eyed the river running alongside the forest's edge. "I love it."

"We always keep the kitchen fully stocked, and I have plenty of clothes stored here, just as I do at the castle." He opened the trunk, grasped her purchases and climbed the front steps. "There's a four-digit key code needed to enter."

"I'll get it for you." She walked up beside him. "What's the number?"

"One, one, one, one."

"Huh?" She frowned, so damn endearingly. "I think you're supposed to use a number no one is supposed to guess."

"Would you have guessed that?"

"No, but that's not the point." She unlocked the door and opened it.

"We like to make things easy if we can." He slid the bags inside then scooped her up before she could enter. "Would you like that shower you missed out on this morning?"

"I'd love one, particularly since I've been rolling around in dirt since." She wrapped her arms around his neck as he carried her over the threshold.

"One shower coming up." He nudged the door shut with his hip and weaved through the large lounge with its four tan leather couches and big screen TV. Down the passageway, across the plush cream carpet, he strode. He passed his brothers' bedrooms then stopped at the open doorway of his own and gently set her back on her feet. "The bathroom is to the side. I'll grab your bags."

"Thank you." She unzipped her knee-high leather boots and peeled them and her socks off then shrugged out of his borrowed shirt and whipped her tank top over her head. A peek of her nipples showed through the sheer white silk of her bra, and her jeans sitting snug on her hips, added to the mouth-watering sight he couldn't turn away from. No, he wouldn't be able to move an inch from this spot even if his life depended on it.

"You were going to get the bags…" Gaze on him, she slid the button of her jeans free, lowered the fly then wriggled the blue denim down her gloriously creamy legs and off. Nothing but two scraps of silk covered her and his cock throbbed to attention and wept for more. "They're by the front door, Iain, where you left them, remember?"

"I know exactly where they are, my mate."

"Then could you choose something from my purchases for me to wear after I've showered?" She sashayed up against him and he wound a lock of her hair around his finger before allowing the silky length to slip free and bounce between her breasts.

"I'd rather you wear nothing."

"I'm sure you would, but I'm not going to." She flounced backward, turned and walked into the bathroom with her pert bottom swaying back and forth. She closed the door and he wanted to hammer it down. Instead, he forced air into his lungs and attempted to get his thoughts back on track. It was time to woo his woman.

He returned to the front door, collected her bags and spread the contents over his bed. He folded everything and stored it all away in the top two drawers of his oak dresser, all but the tiny, two-piece racy-red swimsuit. That he left for her to wear.

Out on the porch, he breathed deep. Time to come up with a plan. He wanted their time together here to be incredibly special. He'd catch some fresh fish for dinner tonight. She'd said she liked it pan-fried. He strode down the steps, crossed the lush meadow and stopped at the river bank. The stream was wide, deep in the middle and shallow where it pooled at each side. He'd spent so many hours out here, allowing his bear to splash about before lumbering out and curling up on the grass to dry in the warm sunshine.

Water gushed over jutting rocks farther downstream where the forest thickened. Each summer, he and his brothers would lug out the canoes from the back shed and paddle to Loch Bear only a few miles distant. There the waters teemed with fish. They'd catch all they needed, row back and cook their haul over an open fire.

"Iain!" Wrapped in a fluffy blue towel, her skin glistening from her shower and her damp hair dripping down her back, Isla waved from the front porch. Barefoot, she skipped across the meadow then stopped before him, her red bikini dangling from one hand. "I got really hot, even with the shower turned to its coldest setting. I need to shift, badly."

"Then I'll join you."

"Are you sure?"

"If you're shifting, so am I." He tossed his leather jacket onto the ground, eased his silver-threaded shirt over his head then shucked his leather pants and slid his thumbs inside the waistband of his black silk boxers. "I don't care to shred any clothes when I shift. I hope you don't mind me stripping completely off."

"I have no issue with that at all, provided you don't mind me doing the same." She dropped her bikini on top of his pile of clothes, her gaze moving over his chest then down his legs. With one lick of her lips, she dropped her towel.

Nothing. She wore not a stitch of clothing, and his bear almost jumped right out of him.

Chapter 6

Across the Highlands, a great distance from the ancient House of Clan Matheson, 1210.

For the past month, from the passing of the last full moon to the rise of tonight's one, Ivan had ridden across the Highlands following the path his soul had led him on. Everything within him now sensed his mate. She was close and his desire to find her beat at him as the night sky above darkened to a midnight black.

Urging his destrier to a faster pace, he bolted along a grassy ridge bathed in the moon's glow and through the darkened forest. He rode hard until he reached a clearing where a mystical stone circle appeared before him, a most magical and sacred place.

The massive slabs of stone shone a serene white, and there, standing in the center of a dozen tall pillars stood a young woman in a corseted cream gown, her pale hair curling in long golden locks down her back. The fine velvet of her gown hugged her trim waist with an entwining of gold and cream silk ribbons along the bodice.

He slowed his horse, pulled up and after dismounting, slung his reins over a low branch of one of the towering pines. The wind whistled around him, buffeting against his padded deerskin cotun and leather pants as he passed through the outer edge of the stone circle and stopped before her. He looked deep into her eyes and drank the sight of her in. "I cannae believe you're here."

"I've felt driven to come to this place this eve." She smiled and tugged the edges of her cream fur cape tighter about her. "Three months past, a seer took refuge within our walls, a wise woman by the name of Nessa. She said this need that burned deep inside me would be because of you."

"Nessa is my grandmother." Three months past, Nessa had

taken several guardsmen with her on a journey of spiritual enlightenment, or so she'd said. Now he knew what that journey had been all about, as well as the secretive smile upon her face when she'd returned. "What did Nessa say to you?"

"She spoke of Gilleoin, that his line is called 'Son of the Bear' and that he was the first man to draw claws and shift, a gift bestowed upon him by The Most High One. This she told me in great confidence, that you would come on this night and claim me as your mate. She assured me I would have naught to worry about, that we were destined for each other."

"Aye, she spoke only the truth." He bowed his head. "My name is Ivan and I'm the second-born son of Gilleoin from the House of Clan Matheson. My soul recognizes and longs for yours just as your soul longs for mine. May I have your name?"

"Lady Bethia, daughter to the Chief of Tainfield Castle. My clan have strong ties to the Royal House of Lorne from the Celtic Kings of Dalriada. Nessa informed me that Gilleoin's lineage too stems from the same Royal House." She motioned through the trees to where a fortress of stony gray rose high. The castle's massive gray tower windows were lit with candlelight, its garrisoned walls topped with battlements and guardsmen patrolling the barbican. "My home."

"Then I would like to speak to your father."

"You may, but he is sickly and plagued with the chills and isnae up to visitors this eve. Nessa told me he would survive his ailment but no' recover his great strength. She said you would be the one to lead our clan in his stead, until my younger brother comes of age. He is but ten and three."

"What else did Nessa say?" His grandmother was a wily woman, one he completely adored.

"There were so many things she knew about me, things that I've never spoken of to another soul." She shuffled closer, until the tips of her white satin slippers touched his booted feet.

"My grandmother came to pave the way for my arrival."

"Aye, she loves you greatly. That I understood well. She also gave me her word you were a man of great honor." An intriguing smile lifted her lips. "Will you show me your other form, that of the bear?"

"'Tis too soon. I dinnae wish to frighten you."

"Your grandmother promised me you'd never be able to do so. And there is naught that frightens me."

"Did she also explain what this night would entail?"

"Aye." A mischievous glint lit her eyes. "That should we complete the bond then we would form an unbreakable merge of the mind. I must warn you though, I've always suffered a rather impetuous streak. I couldnae help but sneak out to meet you afore you arrived at Tainfield's gate. I wanted to speak with you first in private."

"Glad I am then for your rash behavior, and aye, I promise you'll never regret meeting me here." He lowered to one knee, took her tiny hand in his and spoke the words drawn deep from within his soul. "You're my mate, the one woman I wish to share my life with. Will you do me the great honor of becoming my wife?"

"I should insist you speak to my father first."

"Aye, you should." He swung her into his arms and carried her to his horse. "Allow me to take you home."

"I'd rather no' return this eve." She wrapped her arms around his neck, buried her nose in his shoulder-length hair, and whispered, "My answer is aye, I wish to be your wife, and my soul aches for more this very night. I desire the bond and all that it entails."

"As I desire you, to complete the bond and merge fully as one, although we have only just met and I have no issue if you wish to wait."

"Mayhap I forgot to mention my impetuousness?" She smiled, her lips lifting into a playful grin.

"I see." Grinning back, he carefully set her upon his horse, slid in behind her and with his arms around her, slapped his reins against his destrier's neck and rode toward the quaint inn he'd passed at the edge of the forest some miles back.

Tonight was their night, and no other's.

He would woo his mate as she deserved and if she truly wished for more, he would gladly join with her. Bethia was his, now and forever.

Chapter 7

Isla stood unclothed before her mate, her towel lying in a puddle at her feet next to the gurgling river meandering through the forest near his cabin. This was the most beautiful place, so private and secluded and it was just them within this little slice of paradise.

"You should have warned me you were about to do that." Iain, his thumbs still stuck inside the waistband of his black silk boxers, stared into her eyes.

"Do you still intend to shift with me?"

"Absolutely. What my lady asks for, she shall receive." He slid his boxers down his muscled legs then kicked them on top of his pile of clothing. Every inch of him was on delicious display and although she'd touched him earlier in the day, made him come with her hand alone, that time together paled in comparison to the intensity and raw intimacy of this moment.

"Need to touch you." Ragged words as he stepped closer. He trailed a finger down her neck then gently, carefully, he cupped both her breasts, dipped his head and licked one nipple. The heavy rasp of his tongue across sensitive flesh sent a flurry of need pulsing through her core. "I long to make you mine, Isla."

"I'm already yours. I was from the moment I was born." She dropped to all fours and for a miniscule moment, pain seared through her as her bear broke free. The Change was swift and fast, the pain leaving her as quickly as it had come.

Iain grumbled, dropped and in a sizzling display of fireworks, made the Change beside her. One large bear with silky black fur lumbered closer, his beast twice her size as he nudged her muzzle with his own then rose up on his hind legs and roared. His thunderous growl stated his claim, that she was his and for all others to remain far away, not that they weren't already alone.

Grinning, she plodded into the shallow water at the edge of

the river then went deeper and paddled across to the other side. She trod up the far bank, shook the water from her body and sent drops flying. Happiness exploded inside her. This was the most glorious place on Earth. In a patch of sunshine, she sat and rolled onto her side, the grass tickling her muzzle and belly. Such a moment of perfection.

Iain followed in her wake, plopped down beside her and dropped one front paw over her rump, his claws lightly scratching her pelt then with lightning speed, he made the Change, fur retracting and muzzle shortening in a shimmer of bright light until the man lay beside her. He stroked her head and rubbed between her ears. "Your bear is beautiful, Isla."

A purr rumbled from her.

"But I have to touch the woman." He stroked down her body, caressing her soft fur. "Change, little bear. I need you."

Liquid heat rushed through her veins at his gentle touch and she took control and forced the Change. All woman, she arched into him and moaned as he gripped her hands, pressed them over her head and stretched out over top of her, his hard shaft pressing into her hip.

"If you want me to stop, tell me so now," he whispered against her lips.

"There's no stopping what is to come. All I ask is that we take things slowly."

"However slow you need. You'll tell me what you like, or what you don't like. What you'd prefer for me to do, or not do."

"Nothing is off limits. I want to be with you in every way."

"So I can touch you wherever I please?" He released her hands and shuffled down, his warm breath brushing across the heated skin of her belly.

"Aye. Can I touch you too?" She sank her fingers into his soft wavy hair and gasped as he licked around her belly button.

"I demand you do." He nipped in a line upward until his nose brushed the underside of her breasts. He cupped both mounds and thumbed the peaking tips. "I want to taste every inch of you as well."

"I want that too." Boy did she want, and with a desperation she'd never experienced before.

"It feels as if I've waited a lifetime for this moment." He

sucked her nipple deep into his mouth then moved to the other. Heat rippled through her. Then he caught her hand, turned it over and kissed her palm in the sweetest caress. Her heart melted as he lifted his gaze to hers and smiled. "There's something I need to say before we go any further."

"I'm listening."

He laced their hands together. "Isla Matheson, from this day forward, I promise to protect and keep you safe, to honor your needs above my own. All that I am is yours, heart, body and soul."

Tears filled her eyes, and she slid her hand over the heavy beat of his heart. "Iain, you've stolen my will to be anywhere but here with you."

"Good, because from this moment forth, you'll never leave my side." He stroked over the claw-and-star tattoo on her hip, a seriously hungry look lighting his eyes as he gazed at her breasts. He licked one nipple, so sensuously slow. "You taste so sweet." He drew the aureole deep into his mouth and played the tip with his tongue. Oh, he knew exactly how to use his tongue. She palmed the back of his head and held him against her breast as he sucked.

"That feels amazing."

"Tell me if I do anything you don't like." He tugged her onto her side, slid one of his legs between hers, and in a dark, sexy tone, murmured, "Touch me."

She encircled her hand around his thick cock and smiled as a drop beaded and glistened on the plump head. "I want to do more than touch." She slithered down, licked the tip then swirled her tongue around the head. He tasted divine, salty and strong, and she sucked, taking as much of him in as she could. "Mmm, this could get rather addictive, rather quick."

He growled and rocked his hips. "I won't last long if you do that."

"Please, just a little more." She took him deeper, slid her hand lower and cupped his balls covered with a smattering of dark hair. Carefully, she caressed them. He was all hers and soon she'd have the telepathic link their mated couples did. She longed for it.

"Cease. No more." He pulled her up, tumbled her onto her

back and kissed her. His hunger was potent, the same as hers, and his mind, it pounded at the edge of hers as it demanded entrance. "Your scent is driving me insane." Stroking down her sides and over her hips, he nuzzled her mound and breathed deep. Then he spread her legs and revealed all of her to his ravenous gaze. With a rumble, he stroked a finger along her slit. "So wet, and all mine."

"Aye, all yours." She slid her legs against his, her heartbeat a pounding mess. Then he ducked his head and she tangled her hands in his shoulder-length locks. She held onto him as his tongue swept across her flesh, as he extended his claws then retracted and curled his hands around her hips. A firestorm radiated out from where he touched, as he moved his mouth over her sensitive clit, and sucked, hard. "That feels sooo good."

"For me too, but I need more, Isla." Licking her, he built her orgasm to exquisite perfection and she lifted her hips and her legs fell wider. He accepted the invitation, grasped her bottom and drank from her deeper.

Panting, she struggled for a breath at the intense emotions surging through her. "I don't want to come this time without you inside me."

"Are you sure?" He lifted his head, his gaze holding hers.

"Aye."

"Then what my woman wants, she shall receive." He came up over top of her, nipped her lower lip, then with his hands on her hips, he slowly, carefully, moved between her legs and nudged his cock along her slick folds.

She cupped his face, her mind shoving against the barrier still between them. "Do it."

He tore through her barrier below, and as he did, the block between their minds fell away and he lay completely open to her. Her mind tunneled deep inside his and along a private pathway that would only ever be theirs. "*My mate,*" she murmured mind-to-mind as she gripped his shoulders, his cock buried so deep inside her. Never had she felt so completely and wonderfully full.

"*Aye, your mate, always and forever.*" Ever so slowly he slid back out then stopped and pushed all the way back inside her. She clung to him, wanting more, as hard and fast as he could give it yet also wanting it slow so this moment would never end.

"*I can sense your thoughts, Isla. Fast and hard, but also slow so this moment never ends. That shall not be an easy task.*"

"*Start with fast and hard, then we'll get to the slow and never-ending part later.*"

"*As you wish.*" Thrusting, he pounded into her and every nerve ending in her body charged and sparked where they touched. She rocked with him, sucked the skin of his neck between her lips and bit down when she could no longer hold back. She marked him, as territorial as any female bear would. Her man. Her mate.

"*Do that again,*" he growled in her mind, his pace increasing.

She nuzzled the other side of his neck, lapped at his skin then grazed her teeth back and forth. Slowly, succinctly, she bit down and he roared his pleasure, bucked into her and marked her neck in the same way.

"*This feels so good.*" Her lashes fluttered down. "*I don't want to leave your mind.*"

"*Then don't, only look at me. I want to see your pleasure when it comes.*"

She opened her eyes. He was buried so exquisitely deep, and his heartbeat thumped against hers. Then he laid claim to her lips and sent every one of her last thoughts flying. "*Touch me below. I'm so close, Iain.*"

"*Here?*" He touched her clit, so gently.

"*Aye, please, more. Need more.*"

"*This day*"—he caressed her nub—"*I've found my true peace.*" Then he drove deep and her inner muscles tightened and locked him in place. Blissful spasm after spasm racked through her body, each of his possessive strokes a balm to her soul. Then he jerked, his seed shooting inside her, and with the skill of his mouth taking hers, he sent her soaring over the edge once again and far from her body. He'd taken her over, from the inside out and she reveled in it all.

"*Aye, peace.*" She wrapped her arms around his neck and held onto him as her lashes fluttered down.

* * * *

Iain lifted up a little, not wanting to bear his full weight on his woman. He'd wanted her with a thirst he'd never known before, and even though he'd just come, his need for her still raged deep within him. He'd longed for her since the moment their bond had solidified five years ago, and just the thought of the years they'd already lost near tore his heart in two. He wouldn't lose a moment more.

He slid down her body, raised her legs and spread them until she lay even more fully exposed to him.

"What are you doing?" She opened her eyes and rested her elbows underneath her as she peered languorously at him.

"You're so beautiful, so pink and lush." Her soft flesh enticed him and gently, he touched the smear of blood along her inner thighs and reveled in the fact that she'd given him her innocence, the right allowed only to him. It was the most precious gift, one he'd now claimed, just as he'd in turn allow her to claim whatever she wished from him. To his dying day, he would be hers to command. "Do you hurt here?"

"A little." Her golden gaze softened.

"Then allow me to take care of you." He stood and walked into the river, scooped fresh water and returned to her. Tenderly, he washed her clean, and once done, pressed a soft kiss against her bare mound. "I can't believe you're smooth down here."

"I like to wax and keep things tidy, no matter the other half of me sprouts fur."

"I adore your fur, as well as all things smooth." He parted her folds and plunged his tongue deep inside her. She bucked, her nipples hardening into tight points. "Hmm, it appears you like it when I taste you here."

"I have a feeling I'll like everything you do." She gasped for breath. "Surely neither of us can come again so quickly?"

"I'm hungry, Isla. I wish for you to come often, and always at my hand." Lapping her, he eased one finger in then as she mewled for more, a second finger. Gently, he caressed her, her soft cries a heavenly crescendo that made his chest pump out. This was what he wanted, to hear her passion and know it came because of his touch. Sensations stormed through him and his cock throbbed as he imbibed at the very heart of her.

"Iain, that feels so good, but I need your mouth on mine."

He lifted up, took her mouth in a hot kiss as he continued to stroke his fingers into her below. As he did, she caressed his cock with long pulls and his spine tingled as the pressure in his shaft built.

He'd longed for her for so long, to join with her and make her his in every way. Now her sweet demands were driving every rational thought from his head. Kissing her, tasting the delectable recesses of her mouth had his cock begging for release. Soon. There was so much more of her he yet needed.

Still fondling her below, he slid down a little, tracing her skin with his mouth and tongue. He gorged himself on her full breasts, sucking her pebbled nipples deep inside his mouth until she could barely breathe for the pleasure. He feasted on her creamy flesh, licking over her flat belly and along her groin. He nibbled on her inner thighs, first one and then the other, her knees quivering either side of his shoulders. His bear rumbled deep within him, demanding another taste of her, to know her scent and to imbibe.

Blood pounding, he lowered his head to her clit and razzed the tip with his teeth. She was his, always his, and his mind went dark with lust as he smoothed his hands along her inner thighs and opened her up more fully for his touch. He drank her in, allowing his desperate need for her to consume him.

"Iain!" She screamed his name and he raised up and plunged his cock deep inside her, reveling in the fiery heat of her core. "Oh goodness." She clutched his butt and pulled him in even deeper. "You feel so good, like there isn't an inch of me not filled with you."

"There isn't." He lifted up then slowly pushed back in. As he did, his mind swept out along their telepathic link and tightened its hold on her. *"We're one, and always shall be, from this day forth."*

"Make me fly." She kissed him and he pounded harder and deeper.

His thoughts flew as she raked his back then he was lost as her inner muscles tightened and dragged him in. He roared, his release exploding violently along with hers as he spilled his seed deep within her.

Such a perfect union, his soul connecting and locking tight with hers, for all time. Aye, she was his, the only one he'd ever desire.

* * * *

The wave of pleasure sweeping through Isla had her struggling to gain a decent breath. This was heaven, and she never wanted their time together in this special place to end, not now, not ever. Bright flashes of yellow and white still burst behind her closed eyelids as her channel pulsed around Iain's cock, over and over. It was too much, yet not enough. She pushed against his broad shoulders though he moved not an inch. "Roll over. It's my turn on top."

"As you wish." He rolled them smoothly over in the lush grass, every inch of his body still fully aligned with hers, his cock stirring and lengthening within her all over again.

"I love how you feel inside of me." She caressed the corded muscles of his damp chest, lifted up a little and smiled at the sight where they were joined below. So beautiful.

"I love it far more." He cupped her bottom and rocked his hips, his shaft moving deeper.

"Mmm, I can feel every little movement you make." She cradled his face in her hands, lowered her mouth to his and kissed him. "It's the most precious feeling."

"You look glorious on top of me, all smooth skin and full breasts." His golden eyes twinkled. "Ride me."

"I thought you'd never ask." She eased up then sank back down, taking his cock deep into the heart of her. She moaned at the sweet sensation.

"It doesn't hurt?"

"There's no more pain, only pleasure." She leaned forward, her hands either side of his head on the grass as she moved back and forth, faster and faster until a dizzying need built within her core.

"Come as you please. I'm right here with you." He caught her bobbing breasts between his lips and drew one nipple inside his mouth. The tension of need within her wound tighter, and with one decisive flick of his finger over her clit, he sent her soaring from her body.

Writhing, she gave into the whirlpool of emotions taking her. She convulsed around him as she flew, and as she rode the waves, he rolled her onto her back and sank balls-deep inside her. With a fierce bellow, he joined her in paradise.

This moment marked their future.

She would set her past aside and embrace her mate and his clan, her place now at his side, and his at hers. He was the one man she could never live without and as he kissed her, bringing her slowly back down from the heavens she'd transcended to, peace invaded her, to the depths of her soul.

Merged fully as one, he would be hers, for all time.

Chapter 8

One month following Kenneth and Elizabeth's marriage, ancient House of Clan Matheson, 1210.

In the dark of night, Nessa hurried across the inner courtyard through the drizzly cold. Torches mounted on the stone walls spread their flickering glow across the stony ground and up toward the battlements where guardsmen patrolled in battle attire, their weapons holstered at their sides.

She'd known this night would come, when tensions would once again fester and rise between the clans. The MacKenzie clan desired their land and the strategic position they held on the edge of Loch Alsh close to the north-eastern tip of Sleat. The waterways they guarded were a prize to behold and their enemy was well aware of it. Control was what the MacKenzie chief wanted, and what he intended to get.

She stepped inside the front door, untied her black cloak and draped it over her arm as she proceeded toward the great hall. A buzz of voices echoed toward her and she took a deep, fortifying breath and entered the vaulted room with its high wooden beamed rafters and blazing fireplace. Sorcha had already asked the servants to move the trestle tables to the far side of the hall. Sleeping pallets had been laid down to accommodate the additional number of warriors who'd arrived from clan MacDonald to aid them.

She hurried around the hall and knocked on the chief's solar door. "Gilleoin, 'tis I."

"Come in, Nessa."

She entered and closed the door behind her.

Gilleoin sat behind his desk and Kenneth in the padded chair next to the blazing fire.

She walked to the narrow window overlooking the courtyard and gripped the stone windowsill.

"Have you seen aught more?" Gilleoin asked her.

"Aye, my visions are strong this eve. Ivan has arrived safely and found his mate awaiting him." She turned, faced them both. "A vision has also shown me we're about to receive the most interesting aid. Three warriors of immense strength are soon to arrive."

"We'll need more than an additional three sword-hands to win this war."

"These men are unlike any warriors who have come to our shores afore."

"How do you mean?" Kenneth leaned forward, elbows to his knees and the fire's glow lighting the bits of steel studded within his thick brown leather vest.

"They can shift shape and draw claws as you, your brother, and your father can."

"How is that possible?" He shoved to his feet. "Father is the first."

"These three warriors are the 'power of three,' our future as well as our past. If we wish to win this war, to save our people and to give hope to those yet still to come, then we must listen to them well. Far into the future, they are all that we shall become."

Aye, the prophecy was in motion, and very soon, the 'power of three' would be unveiled.

Chapter 9

Bottom snug in the curve of her mate's groin, Isla lay curled on her side in Iain's king-size bed two weeks following their first joining. Never had she awoken more content and rested in her life. Here at their cabin, they'd made love every day, lazed together by the river and fished and tramped. They'd bonded so strongly, their merged link now a rich entwining of their minds and her love for him so deep, it hurt just to walk a few steps from his side.

She wriggled around and squinted as the morning sunshine streamed through the sheer white nets and played its lacy pattern over the wooden beamed walls of his room. The partially opened window blew the nets inward and circulated Scotland's freshest air, but it was his warm woodsy pine scent that overrode it all and made this space so heavenly.

"If you're awake," he murmured, eyes closed as a ray of sunshine played over the vivid midnight-black of his shoulder-length locks and across his high cheeks, "then I demand my morning kiss."

She trailed one finger along his jaw then over the sharply defined cleft in his chin. She kissed the delectable indent then nipped his bottom lip. His breathing changed and her smile widened. "I'm going to take a shower. Care to join me?"

"Hell, yes." He slowly opened one eye. "There is nothing I love more than seeing your skin flush under the heat of the water."

"It's not the hot water that causes the flush." She shoved the forest-green leafed bedcovers back and skipped into the bathroom. The lovely rich colors of gold and cream greeted her, as well as a massive mirror along one wall, which reflected the bedroom and Iain already standing guard at her back, his gorgeous body on stunning display and making her ache for him all over again. "I'm not sure I'm going to be able to return to civilization today."

"I've kept you all to myself for a fortnight now and my clan will descend on us if we don't show ourselves soon." He reached past her, opened the glass shower door, turned the lever on and stuck his hand under the water. "This is a perfect temperature."

"I'm nervous about meeting your parents. I ran for so long."

"You had your reasons, ones even I understand, and they will adore you. It will be impossible for them not to." He walked her backward into the shower and closed the door. The water sluiced through her hair and down her body as he pinned her against the side, one hand planted beside her head on the glass, the other curled around her nape.

Hot water pummeled his shoulders as she slid her arms around his neck and held on. "I love the way you hold me. It makes me feel so cherished and grounded. And when you're inside me, I can feel your strength and the most exquisite tenderness." She hooked one leg behind his knee, rubbed up and down his calf. These past two weeks, he'd stolen her will to be anywhere but with him.

"I intend for you to feel far more than cherished. I want to see to your every desire." He whispered the words as steam swirled around them.

"Can you tell what I desire right now?" She nibbled his neck and heat flooded her below, making her wetter than she already was.

He breathed deep, scenting the air then grinned and cupped her bottom. He lifted her up, pressed himself hard against her. "I have a very good idea. I want inside of you, now."

With one hand, she grasped his shaft and rubbed the plump head against her folds. His already hard cock got incredibly harder, then he slid her down over top of him, and he filled her, so slowly, so completely.

She gasped at their delicious joining then got lost in a storm of sensation as he took her hard and fast, the way she needed, the way her mind whispered to his in demand for. He pumped into her and her inner muscles gripped and pulled him in even deeper. Then she kissed him and he took her frantically, as unable to hold back in his desire as she was in hers. Soaring, she tumbled over the edge of no return, just as he roared his satisfaction and joined her in their own little slice of paradise.

Aye, two weeks alone with him wasn't nearly long enough.

* * * *

"I can't believe we must leave." Except their duties called and after a late breakfast, Isla packed her belongings in the suitcase Iain had fetched from the hallway cupboard and zipped it up. She'd left a few things in the top drawer of his oak dresser, enough for when they stayed over, but the remainder she'd take with her to Ivanson Castle.

"Allow me to aid you." Iain clutched the handle and lifted her bag off the bed. He'd dressed in a white shirt, the cuffs rolled to his elbows and his clan kilt belted at his waist. He looked every lip-licking inch a delectable Highland warrior with daggers sheathed at each wrist and a sword at his side.

"One thing I am looking forward to is watching you train." She smoothed her hands through his hair and tidied his drying locks as best as she could. Finlay had sent him a message and told him to come prepared to battle when he returned. "I've always wanted to wield a sword, but my father wouldn't permit it. Instead he taught me how to shoot an arrow and I have a near perfect aim at a hundred yards."

"We hold an archery competition in the spring. Many of our women compete as well. You too should. You'll have fun. I'm sure of it." Holding her hand, he led her down the hallway, through the lounge and out the front door. He carried her bag to the SUV and stowed it inside the trunk.

She keyed in the door's lock sequence, trekked down the steps and lifted her face skyward. The odd puffy white cloud floated across the vivid blue sky and birds soared above, dipped then landed on the highest branches of the towering trees at the forest's edge. The river ran swifter today after the rain that had fallen yesterday and farther downstream, water gushed around thick boulders and flowed around the bend. The grass grew lusher, greener, and the wildflowers across the meadow bobbed their pretty heads at her as she walked to where Iain held her door open for her. "I'll miss this place."

"We'll return as often as we're able to."

"Is it wrong of me to still want you all to myself?" She eased inside the passenger seat and secured her seat belt.

"No, I feel the same way about you." Iain drove along the

bumpy dirt track then turned onto the private gravel road leading toward the castle. The forest stood thick and strong around them, and within a short time the stone walls of the keep rose up ahead. They parked in the large lot at the rear, one filled with dark SUVs and the odd sports car. Iain's red convertible gleamed where it had been parked near the rear row of pines.

"Someone cleaned your car."

"Kirk would have. The blue ride next to mine is his and he can't stand seeing any grit on either of our girls." He collected her bag and guided her through the postern gate. On the battlements above, two men wearing leather vests over dark shirts and pants lifted a hand toward him and he waved back.

They continued on, around the perimeter of the inner bailey and past a dozen men in belted kilts and white shirts, swords in hand as they trained. Finlay and Kirk were amongst them, sweat glistening on their skin as they swung at each other, steel clashing loud against steel.

"It looks like I'm just in time." Iain set her case down near the front steps leading into the keep and palmed the hilt of his sword. "If you'd like, stay and watch."

"I'm definitely watching, and be careful." She lifted onto her toes and kissed his chin. "No one is allowed to hurt you, and if they do, they'll have me to answer to."

"I'll be sure to inform one and all." He clasped her jean-clad hips, rubbed his body against hers and marked her with more of his delectable scent.

"You are one territorial bear."

"It can't be helped." Grinning, he backed away, removed his sword from its sheath and strode toward his brothers. He warmed up, swinging his blade in a wide figure eight. His shoulders and arms, so thick and strong, were packed with muscle and she'd adored every inch of them this past fortnight. She couldn't have asked for a more precious time with him.

Luckily her duties for her own clan were being taken care of by Daniel.

Finlay eyed Iain as he advanced, his weapon held high. "About time you turned up."

"You sound mad, and you also appear rather on edge." Iain jumped into the fray and brought his weapon down on Finlay's.

"What's up?"

"I've had trouble with my bear these last couple of days." Finlay battled him, landing one hard blow after another. "He's getting antsy, clawing for the next full moon. I've already shifted twice today to calm him. Kirk's in much the same fierce mood."

"Fierce would be putting it mildly." Kirk struck Iain and the clash of their blades clanged around the yard.

"Hey!" she called out. "No hurting my mate."

"Aye, I should warn you both." Iain swung at Kirk. "No one is permitted to hurt me. Orders from my chosen one."

"Good to see you're back, Iain." Across the yard near the armory, a man in his mid-forties wearing tan trousers with a chunky black belt and a dark button-down shirt, strode toward Iain and his brothers, a glinting blade in his hand. A woman walked at his side dressed in a pleated blue skirt and a cream blouse, her wavy black hair swaying in a soft bob on her shoulders. The man had to be Michael, Iain's father. The similarities between him and the three battling brothers were too striking for him not to be.

Her phone buzzed and she pulled it from her pocket and answered it. "Hey."

"Hey back at ya." Daniel's deep voice rolled over her, made her miss home. She'd had the odd call from him and Dad, each time insisting they were fine. They'd both updated her on the Mathie case each time they'd rung. Keeping her in the loop was important, not that they'd had any new information other than that Owen and Ewan Mathie still remained under the radar.

"How are Emma and the baby?"

"Emma's just taken our little boy to the doc for his eight-week checkup and she won't be back for another hour. Where are you now?"

"I've just returned to Ivanson Castle but I need some time to get to know Iain's parents and clan. I'm coming home in another week. Let Dad know for me." She leaned against the stone wall, in the cool of its shadow and rubbed one sweaty palm on her jean-clad leg.

"You sound a little nervous."

"I ran from their son for five years. What's not to be nervous about?"

"I met them when I scouted out your new digs. They weren't condemning of you at all when we spoke, only excited that Iain had finally found you."

The woman next to Michael with the soft bob walked past a center well trailed in ivy. She was headed on a direct course toward her.

"I have to go. It appears I can't hide out any longer."

"Sure, but take care, and don't fight the pull."

"Don't fight what p—" A beeping sounded in her ear. Daniel had hung up on her. Unusual.

Iain's mother stopped before her, her smile radiant. "Welcome to Ivanson Castle. I'm Megan."

"I—ah—I'm sorry for the anguish I caused you and your kin these past five years. I mean, this is a momentous moment for me, meeting you."

"There's nothing to be sorry about, and I knew Iain would eventually find you. Everything happens in its own time and usually for a very good reason, something I've learnt well over the years." Megan squeezed her hands and looked into her eyes. "Iain was so determined to find you, just as his brothers have been in their search for their mates. They long for what Iain has now gained, a strong and loving woman at his side."

"Thank you." Megan's words touched her heart.

"Are you all right?" Iain met Kirk's hard strike then darted a look at her. *"Come out of the shadows, love. I'm about to lose my focus with you out of my sight. My brothers will soon notice my distraction and take advantage of it."*

She stepped into the sunshine. *"Is that better?"*

"Infinitely." His sexy grin made her heartbeat pound.

Finlay and Kirk circled him.

"Watch out. Your brothers are preparing for a dual attack. Keep your eyes on them, not on me."

"You're a far more appealing sight than them."

His brothers advanced from opposite sides.

Finlay mouthed to Kirk, "Three, two, one."

Their blades descended.

Iain spun his sword high and blocked both well-timed blows with one swing. He dropped low, kicked Finlay off balance then swept his other leg out and knocked Kirk in the shin.

Both his brothers fell into a heap on the ground.

Iain eyed her as he breathed deep. "*I miss you.*"

"*I miss you too.*"

Finlay and Kirk jumped back to their feet and returned to the fight.

All around Iain the other men partnered together battled hard. Some had shucked their shirts and their chests glistened with sweat as gravel dust rose and clouded the air. They wielded their swords in a battle of strength against one another, a stunning sight to see.

"We can go closer if you wish?" Megan touched her arm. "Once one has bonded, the desire to be near each other grows from strength to strength. I know the best place where Iain will be able to keep an eye on you without his ability to battle being affected, not that it appears that way at the moment. He's holding his own."

"Thank you. I'd like that." She walked with Megan around the perimeter of the courtyard toward the curtain wall closest to Iain and sat beside Megan as she perched on a wooden slatted bench just out of reach of the dappled shade of a large elm tree.

"I'm glad you've had the past two weeks alone with him." Megan crossed her legs as she rested back on the bench. "He'll be at far more peace now having had the chance to strengthen your bond before the daily grind of business takes over again."

"I'm aware your clan takes on government contracted cases similar to ours."

"Aye, Daniel, when he visited two weeks ago, mentioned the similarities as well, although your clansmen utilize your fae skills to their best advantage while our clansmen must rely on their increased shifter strength alone."

"Did Daniel show you his ability?"

"No, what skill does he hold?"

"Telekinesis. He can immobilize a threat by levitation. It's rather interesting to watch him hang a man upside down in midair, and depending on his mood, spin him around."

"Oh, how intriguing." She clapped and giggled. "He'll have to show me the next time he visits. I'm most fascinated by your ability to compel. The guardsman you slipped past when you first left couldn't even recall having met you."

"I compelled that request of him. Ordinarily though, I don't use my skill against my own kin, other than for training purposes. One of my father's rules and we all try to adhere to it." A rule she'd apply here at her new home too.

"Tell me more about your father. I'm aware you lost your mother not long after you were born. Daniel mentioned it, and that you're very close to your father."

"Dad did the most amazing job raising me, although I've never been without female guidance. Our clan is tight and I consider many of the older women strong motherly figures." She rolled her shoulders and rested back as Megan had done. "Dad definitely still suffers from her death though, and now I'm mated, I can truly understand why." If she lost Iain it would kill her. That she knew to the depths of her soul. Across the courtyard, he fought hard, his sculpted chest and honed muscles rippling under the thin white cotton of his billowy shirt. *"I want to roll around in bed with you, like right now."*

He stumbled, righted himself and slammed his blade into Finlay's. *"Give me ten more minutes and I'm there. I have to at least shake some of this restlessness out of my brothers."*

"Ten minutes, and I'm holding you to that. I have some restlessness you need to shake out of me too."

Megan straightened one of the pleats in her ankle-length blue skirt. "Those who wish to survive following their mate's passing must have strong kinship bonds in place to hold them to the here and now. We'll ensure your father never loses you."

"Losing him has always been one of my greatest fears. Iain's promised me I can return home as often as I need to and I'm very grateful for that."

Finlay and Kirk growled as they swung at each other, their strikes becoming harder and fiercer with each blow. Megan eyed her sons and frowned. "Something is truly up with those two. I've never seen Finlay and Kirk so aggressive. Both have had to shift twice today already, their bears riding them hard."

"Iain told me their search for their mates seems otherworldly. They follow their senses, yet no matter if they're standing in the very spot where their women should be, there's no one about."

"That's correct."

"I mentioned the details to my father while we were at the cabin, but I haven't heard back if he's had any visions surrounding them yet. Give me a couple of minutes and I'll call him and check in." Cell phone in hand, she wandered underneath the tree, rested back against the trunk and jabbed in Dad's number. Iain watched her as he trained, his golden gaze firm on hers.

"Isla." Dad's voice reverberated down the line. "How are things?"

"Hey, Dad. Things are good. We're back at Ivanson Castle and I just met Iain's mother. I have a question." The breeze rose and the leaves on the elm tree rustled. One drifted free and swirled toward her. She plucked it out of the air and fingered the golden-tinged leaf.

"One moment. Let me find a quiet place to speak to you." His footsteps echoed down the line. A door closed then the familiar sound of his black leather chair creaked as it welcomed his weight.

"Are you in your solar?"

"I am. Shoot me your question."

"It's about Finlay and Kirk's search for their mates. Have you seen anything yet? Do you have even an inkling about what's going on?"

"Iain and his brothers have one of the strongest bonds I've ever seen between siblings, and regarding their mates, it shall be you and not me who ultimately guides them in the right direction." He cleared his throat. "Isla, there's something I must say before it becomes too late."

"Too late for what?"

"You mustn't fight the pull."

"Have you been talking to Daniel?"

"I must warn you. You'll soon be gone and I'll have no way of reaching you for some time. Just know that I love you and we'll see each other again soon. It's time for the 'power of three' to be—"

"Dad?" Her phone beeped and she tapped it, her connection with him gone. Stupid signal.

She called his number, the wind rising and whipping her

hair about her face.

Across the bailey, Iain sheathed his sword and sprinted toward her. He yelled something to his brothers over his shoulder and something lashed at her and tore her merged link with him away. A mist rose and lights shimmered all around. It was as if the stars themselves had escaped the sky and blazed above.

Clutching her belly, she fell away into a dark abyss. "No!" Her scream reverberated through the dense fog, ringing in her own ears.

Chapter 10

Thunder boomed and lightning slashed within the pitch black. The wind shoved and twirled Isla around. She searched frantically for her link to Iain but got nothing. Dad had said he'd have no way of reaching her until she returned. Heart pounding, she screamed for her mate. "Iain!"

Hands grabbed at her, hauled her up against a hard male body. "I've got you."

She shoved her hair out of her face and stared into her man's beautiful golden eyes then sank into his mind and clung to him. "What's happening?"

"All I saw was a tunnel of wind churning around you then you were gone. I dived into the vortex that sucked you away."

Finlay and Kirk flew toward them and each one clasped Iain's arms. They surrounded her, covering her back and keeping her in the middle of the three of them.

"Are you all right?" Finlay yelled over the rush of wind to her.

"I am now you're all here. Dad said I'd soon be gone and he'd have no way of reaching me until I returned. He said it's time for the 'power of three' to be unveiled, or at least he almost got that all out."

"Hey, we're slowing down." Kirk stared through the dark, dense fog. Lights once again flickered then an unearthly force sucked them apart and they plummeted into the frigid depths of a loch. Icy water closed over her head and she kicked upward through the murkiness and broke the surface. White-capped waves, lit a silvery hue by the moon high above, broke over her.

She gulped in great drafts of air as Finlay and Kirk surfaced. *"Iain, I'm on the surface."*

"Almost there. Don't move."

Dizziness overwhelmed her and she grabbed her head. Everything went dark and wavered before her eyes. *"Need you, now."*

* * * *

Iain emerged from the loch's dark depths in a fizz of bubbles. Waves sloshed into Isla and she slumped forward into Finlay. His brother seized her waist and held her up.

"Isla!" He powered toward her, hauled her into his arms and lifted one hand to her mouth. Her breath whispered gently in and out and warmed his palm. "She's breathing. I need to get her to land."

"We appear to be close." Finlay pointed over Iain's shoulder. "Behind you."

Across the choppy moonlight waves, a castle rose like a sentinel in the dark, its massive gray stone turrets and towering walls topped with battlements and guardsmen roaming the ramparts. From the multitude of square windows, candlelight flickered as it did in the days of old. "Where the hell are we?"

"We're certainly no longer at Ivanson Castle." Kirk treaded water next to him. "There're so many birlinns moored in the bay. Boats haven't been made like that in a very long time."

At least half a dozen birlinns were roped to the sea-gate landing and bobbed with the incoming tide.

Isla moaned and stirred in his arms. "Iain?"

"I'm here." He pressed a kiss to her forehead. "Wake up, love."

She blinked her eyes open then clutched his shirtfront. "You need to stop disappearing."

"You're the one who disappeared."

"Where are—" She gasped as she stared toward land. "It's Matheson Castle."

"Your home?"

"Aye, although it's so very different. I've seen old sketches depicting it like this. Dad has one hanging in his solar that he drew from a vision he'd had." She glanced at Finlay and Kirk, their dark hair plastered to their faces and necks. "I'm home, or at least as my home appeared in the past. This is the ancient House of Clan Matheson."

"You're saying we've traveled through time?" Finlay shook his head. "Incredible."

"In the future the sea-gate is farther to the right where the water is deeper." She swung her gaze toward a village nestled along the land where it jutted to a point within the inland channel. Smoke curled into the air from several thatch-roofed houses. Cloistered tightly together, they were surrounded by a stone wall. "The village stands. It burnt to the ground in the twelve-hundreds when the MacKenzies landed on our shores and attempted to take the waterways between us and the Isle of Skye. That place is sacrosanct and remains bare except for a commemorative stone laid in honor of all those who lost their lives during the great feud of that time."

"The MacKenzies are an allied clan of Matheson. Why would they burn the village down?" Never once during Iain's travels on the night of a full moon had his senses ever led him here. So too his ancestor had never once spoken of the place he'd called home. The location had been kept a secret due to the prophecy.

"I can assure you we weren't allies with the MacKenzies during the early twelve-hundreds when they attempted to take what was ours."

"I've never heard of this war."

"The Chief of MacKenzie wanted to rule these waterways. Our land sits in the prime position on the tip of Loch Alsh between the mainland and the MacDonald of Sleat's land on the Isle of Skye. The MacKenzie chief wanted to take it all, and he attacked at the heart of our clan to do so. At the time, the MacDonalds joined forces with us to hold the MacKenzies at bay, but the additional number made no difference when they struck. The blackest day in our history was on June the eleventh, twelve-hundred and ten. That's the day we lost the village and so many of our fae skilled people in the fires that burned."

"Tell me all that you can about the village."

"In the nine-hundreds, the faerie king's youngest son visited the village along the loch and fell in love with the chief's daughter."

"I'm aware of that. He wed the lass and their offspring were gifted in the way of the faerie folk."

"Aye, and during Gilleoin's time, after he was bestowed by The Most High One with the ability to shift, he sought out his mate and was led by the full moon to the village. He claimed Sorcha as his, Nessa's daughter, the seer who spoke the prophecy. Sorcha held the skill of aura reading and could perceive another's true intentions. They completed the bond and formed a link of the mind." Isla shivered as she eyed the shoreline. "We'll need to head in. We've no other choice."

"I agree. Let's go." Finlay struck out first. "We're kin and that should count for something."

Kirk fell in on the other side of Isla and together they swam in a close group. As a large wave crested, they rode it in and at knee-depth, slogged through the water into shore.

A warrior wearing a thick brown leather vest studded with bits of steel and a massive claymore holstered across his back marched toward them, several of his men at his flank. He halted and eyed him. "Ye wear the Matheson plaid. I'll have your names."

The warrior's brogue was far thicker than his. He'd have to take care with his words. Easing in front of Isla, water sluicing to his booted feet, Iain palmed the hilt of his belted sword. "I'm Iain Matheson, the Chief of Matheson's eldest son, and we come in peace." He motioned to his brothers who stood either side of him. "This is Finlay and Kirk."

"Ah, I see." He nodded with a smile. "I was informed of your impending arrival, that you're here to aid us in our coming battle against the MacKenzies. My name is Kenneth and I am the firstborn son of Gilleoin." The warrior turned his gaze on Isla. "And who is the lass ye protect?"

"Isla, the eldest daughter of Murdock Matheson, the chief of her clan. And who exactly informed you of our arrival?"

"My grandmother, Nessa. She is the seer of our clan. Come, you've naught to fear from any of us. I'm well aware of where you're from. Nessa and Gilleoin also await your presence in the chief's solar." The warrior led the way across the pebbly beach toward the grassy path winding upward to the castle, his men stepping aside and allowing them safe passage through.

"Well, this is a rather interesting turn of events." Isla rubbed her arms and Iain tucked her under his shoulder as they trekked up the rise, protecting her from the brisk sea breeze as best as he could.

"Nessa did first speak the prophecy." He walked through the arched gates and past flickering torches mounted against the

bailey's stone walls.

Isla's gaze darted around the inner courtyard and she smiled at him. *"Wow. This is amazing to see the castle as it first was. It's also wonderful to have finally brought you home."*

"Perhaps you missed the part about which century this is."

"I minor technicality." She wiped her face with her wet shirtsleeve. Her jeans clung to her legs, outlining every delectable inch. Swiftly, he hauled his white shirt over his head and drew it over hers. The hem dangled around her knees. Better, much better. *"Thanks."* She squeezed his fingers. *"Dad saw that this was about to happen, us traveling through time. I know he did."*

"He should have given us more warning. He and I will have a long talk the moment we return." His boots squelched with water as he entered the great hall with its vaulted ceilings and high wooden beamed rafters. The walls were covered with large tapestries, of hunting and landscape scenes, and the trestle tables had been pushed to one side and dozens of sleeping pallets laid down before the roaring fire. Warriors bedded down for the night, those wearing both Matheson and MacDonald clan plaids.

Kenneth led them toward a side room and opened the door. "Chief, our guests have arrived." He motioned toward Iain. "This is Iain, the Chief of Matheson's eldest son, and the lass is Isla, the eldest daughter of Murdock Matheson, the chief of her clan."

Before a chunky wooden desk, a middle-aged man eased out of his chair and stood in tan pants and a thick fur vest, a sword sheathed at his side. He walked around his desk, plucked a tartan blanket from the corner chair next to the blazing fire and passed it to Iain. "For the lass."

"She is no' just a lass, Gilleoin, but his chosen one." An older woman standing before the narrow window overlooking the courtyard, her red hair wisped with gray and coiled high atop her head, crossed to them in an elegant olive gown with lacy white sleeves fluttering over her wrists. "You've traveled far this day, and I take it, rather unexpectedly. I'm Nessa."

"Iain, and these are my brothers, Finlay and Kirk." Draping the tartan over Isla's shoulders, he gestured toward them with a tip of his head. "I'm glad you're aware of where we've come from. Having to explain how we arrived would have been interesting."

"Aye, I've informed Gilleoin and Kenneth that you've crossed time in order to fulfill the prophecy, the foretelling I decreed at the birth of Gilleoin's sons." She smiled at Isla, her hands folded in front of her. "I've 'seen' your skill to compel, and that your father is the seer, Murdock. 'Tis a rare skill you hold amongst those with fae blood."

"I'm the only compeller in my time. My great grandmother held the skill before me." Swamped in the plaid, Isla wriggled one hand free and threaded her fingers through his. "Can you tell us why we're here, Nessa?"

"In completing the bond with your mate, you fulfilled the prophecy. *'Gilleoin's sons will separate when they come of age and rule their own clans, yet there will come a time far in the future when a mated bond forms between the two clans. Only then must Gilleoin's descendants once again merge, and the 'power of three' be unveiled.'*" Her dark blue eyes swirled with such wisdom within.

"What exactly is the 'power of three?'" Isla stroked the inside of his palm with her thumb. "That's never been made clear within the prophecy."

"Then I shall enlighten you. The 'power of three' are the three brothers who stand in this very chamber. Together, with their chosen ones, they shall instill new blood into the clans and give your future people hope." She moved toward Iain's brothers. "Finlay, Kirk, I'm aware you feel the pull of the full moon toward your women, yet when you search for them you're led to a place where you cannae find them. That is because they are here, in this time, and on the night of the next full moon, on June the fourteenth, the ones you desire shall no longer remain beyond your grasp."

"If they're here in this time then where exactly are they?" Finlay demanded.

"The vision I've received of them still remains hazy. I dinnae always see all, even though I wish it, although I am aware they hold a touch of fae blood as many of the villagers do."

"You're saying our mates await us at the village?"

"Possibly, or they may have traveled farther away. No' all of those who are fae-blooded remain at the village."

"What day have we arrived?" Finlay asked.

"'Tis June the first, the year of our Lord, twelve-hundred and ten, and you've arrived at a time when the MacKenzies are about to descend on us. Their intention is to destroy all that we are, to take our land and the lives of our people, possibly even your mated ones. I'm unsure."

"The village falls on June the eleventh." Isla stepped up to Nessa. "The full moon won't have risen before then."

"Aye, I'm aware of the difficulties that will cause." Tears shimmered in Nessa's eyes. "I give you all my word, that I will remain diligent and watchful. If I see aught more, I shall tell you."

"We can't allow the village to fall." Isla shook her head at Nessa. "Too many innocent people will die."

"I've pleaded with all those at the village to seek shelter here within these walls, or even to move deeper into the sanctuary of the forest, but they are convinced now they've heard my warning they can adequately prepare for an attack and ensure with the use of their skills that they'll be saved." She lowered her head. "I cannae fail my people and I will remain with them in the days ahead. On the morrow, with Gilleoin and Sorcha, I shall return to the village. Even Kenneth has pleaded with them. He holds the ability of death-warning. Of those who live but are soon to die, he receives a vision and with his skill can save those who perish unjustly afore their time. He travels to the village daily and walks amongst them, cautioning and imploring all." She lifted her head. "When I saw your arrival earlier this eve, my vision was strong and provided me with a clear path of understanding. If we wish to win this coming war, then 'tis the 'power of three' that we shall need. The MacKenzies are coming and they are strong."

Finlay growled under his breath. "I won't allow the MacKenzies to slaughter my mate, nor will I allow them to take the lives of innocent people. Gilleoin." He eyed the chief. "You have my sword-hand, however you need it."

"As you have mine." Kirk clasped Finlay's shoulder with one hand and Iain's with the other.

"And of course you have mine." Iain would never allow his brothers to lose their mates. "If we battle, we do so together, as we always have."

"Then I accept your offer with great thanks." Gilleoin's claws burst from his fingertips and lengthened. A fierce growl rumbled from him then he gritted his teeth. "We are the Mathesons, 'Son of the Bear,' and we will stand strong."

* * * *

They would stand strong, and together as one. Isla too wouldn't allow Finlay and Kirk to lose their mates, nor allow the villagers to lose their lives.

Gilleoin marched to the door, claws retracting. He opened it and called out to a maid sweeping the floors. "We have guests. Ensure they're given food and whatever clothing they require. Unfortunately, they've lost all they traveled with." To Iain, he said, "My people are trustworthy. They will never speak to any beyond our own of where you've truly come from."

"I'd appreciate that."

"For now, we'll eat and talk more, devise a plan of attack and whatever else is required to win this war. Nessa has seen we'll need your aid, and I shall gladly accept it." He glanced at Nessa. "See to Mistress Isla's care. She still shivers and I willnae have her suffer a chest illness."

"Of course." Nessa cupped Isla's elbow. "Come with me, my dear. I'll have a chamber prepared for you. I also have a need to speak to you in private, if you dinnae mind."

"One moment." She eyed Iain. *"Is that all right?"*

"Of course. Warm yourself and I'll be with you as soon as I'm able." He brushed a kiss across her forehead. *"Finlay and Kirk's frustration rides them hard."*

"Then stay with them for as long as you need to. I understand." She nodded at Nessa. "Lead the way."

Nessa guided her around the perimeter of the great hall toward the stairwell then slowed as a maid walked toward her in a brown kirtle and a frilly white cap. "Effie, I need you to prepare a bath for Mistress Isla and be as quick as you can about it. She's to have the burgundy chamber next to mine. Bring some gowns from my ambry, and a tray."

"Aye, my lady." The girl dashed upstairs.

"This way." Nessa guided her up the winding stairs and along a dimly lit passageway. Up ahead, two lanky lads with their shirttails fluttering loose over their breeches heaved a tub through a doorway.

They entered the chamber and the lads shuffled out. Across the room, Effie knelt at the hearth, coaxing the sparks of a welcoming fire into life. She added a log and it crackled and caught alight. Rising, she dusted her hands against her aproned sides then bobbed her head and quietly closed the door behind her as she left.

"I can barely comprehend all that's happened in such a short time." Isla removed the tartan blanket she'd snuggled in, her clothes already half dry underneath, then laid it on the end of the four-poster bed with its rich burgundy velvet canopy and crossed to the fire. She rubbed her hands before the blazing warmth. This was real. They'd traveled through time to the past and now had a formidable mission ahead of them.

"Dinnae fear." Nessa gripped her hands. "You hold great strength and courage. You wouldnae have been the one chosen along with your mate to bring Kenneth and Ivan's lines together otherwise."

"Thank you."

"I speak only the truth." She squeezed her fingers. "The words I needed to speak privately to you about. The portal. It couldnae have opened until you'd completed the bond as prophesized, and then of course, conceived a babe. That is the only true sign that proves the two lines had in fact fully merged."

"Conceived a, ah—" She shook her head. "Fertility rates are down in our clans, and I'm only a day or two late at most. Are you sure?"

"You are the daughter of a seer. I would only ever speak the truth with you, just as your father would do the same. I'm sure you're aware you must now take great care. 'Tis too dangerous for a woman who is with child to shift."

"No shifting while pregnant. I'm aware." She fluttered a hand over her belly as a strange surge of protectiveness welled within her. A precious new life grew and she was now responsible for it.

Isla? What's wrong?

Nothing. I just received some unexpected news is all. I'll tell you as soon as you're finished down there.

"Are you sure? I can sense your unease."

"I'm positive." She faced Nessa. "Thank you for telling me."

"Your mate longs to have many babes with you. I've seen such." Nessa wrapped her warm fingers around hers. "Your father too longs for grandchildren. Murdock is a wise seer, and while you are here, I shall watch over you and yours just as your father would wish it."

"Thank you."

A knock sounded and Nessa released her and bid the servants to enter.

Two maids and two lads hustled forward, each carrying a steaming pail of water. Effie returned and hung an armful of gowns in the burgundy curtained ambry, while another lass carried a tray and set it on the side table.

Nessa oversaw the filling of the tub then added a few drops of scented vanilla oil. After the servants left, she shut the door and patted the chair in front of the table. "Come. There's a warm meal and you must eat. Your babes will need to grow to full strength."

"Babes? Hold on." Surely she couldn't mean she was expecting more than one child. "What do you mean by babes?"

A wide smile lifted her lips. "Multiple births run through both Gilleoin and Sorcha's lines. Two or three babes can be birthed at once. 'Tis more difficult, but still it can and is done."

"You need to be more specific. Are we talking two, or three babes?" She plopped onto the chair in front of the side table. Steam from the bowl of chunky seafood stew wafted around her. It smelt delicious and made her belly rumble.

"Eat first then I shall tell you." Nessa sat beside her and passed her a slice of crusty bread.

"Obviously I'm going to need the fortification." She dipped the bread and took a hearty bite. Warmth raced to her belly and calmed her anxiety. "I'm ready."

"There shall be two. Both your sons shall be tangled together and neither older than the other when they are delivered." She raised a brow. "In the future, I've seen that babes can be delivered in a way that remains impossible in this time."

"You mean by caesarean?"

"Aye, that is it." She smiled. "That is how you must deliver them once you've returned, for there is a reason why they must enter the world as one. They shall, one day far into the future, lead together. They are both seers, and their need to merge the clans will be their greatest desire, just as it shall be yours and Iain's. Allow your father to aid in their guidance, to teach them all they need to know of their skill." She crossed to the tub, knelt and swirled her hand through the water. "This is the perfect heat. Come and have your bath."

"I'd love one." She shed Iain's shirt, her blouse then shucked her jeans and stepped into the tub. She lowered into the water, dunked her head and when she emerged, accepted the bar of soap Nessa passed her. She lathered and worked the vanilla scented suds gently through her hair.

At the side table next to the basin and jug, Nessa picked up a brush and knelt at the edge of the tub. "Dip and rinse and I'll untangle your hair for you. 'Tis been whipped into a mighty mess by the portal's strength."

"Thank you. I'd appreciate the help." She went down and popped back up.

Nessa carefully separated her hair into sections then brushed each one.

She relaxed back, resting her head against the wooden rim as she palmed her belly. She stroked in a slow circle as so many emotions swelled inside her. Love, need, desire. She'd give her children what she'd never had, a mother to look after and care for them throughout all of their days.

"I've finished." Nessa rose. "There is still much to be done this eve and I must return to the chief's solar." She passed her a cloth then enveloped her hair in another and rubbed. "Will ye be all right on your own?"

"Of course." She stood, stepped out of the tub and wrapped herself in the cloth. "I understand why you must go."

"Aye, I imagine you do. A seer has little idle time." Nessa crossed to the engraved wooden trunk underneath the narrow window, foraged through it then plucked out an ankle-length nightgown and handed it to her.

She tugged the white linen shift over her head as a knock sounded.

"That'll be the maids." Nessa opened the door and allowed the lads and maids from earlier to clear everything away. Once done, Nessa kissed her cheek. "I shall see you in the morn, my dear. If you have need of me though, my chamber is right across the passageway from yours."

"Thank you." She closed the door behind Nessa with a soft snick, perched on the corner chair before the fire and brushed her hair until it gleamed a silky rich brown. She was here in the past and she'd make sure she used this time gifted to her to do all she could to save the fae villagers. They were her kin just as greatly as Gilleoin's people were.

With her hair dry, she set the brush down on the side table, heaved the thick fur covers on top of the bed back and climbed in.

So much had happened so quickly her head still spun.

Rolling to her side, she burrowed into the soft mattress. "*I miss you.*"

"*I'm coming now. Finlay and Kirk have chosen to sleep on pallets in the great hall amongst the other warriors rather than accept a chamber above-stairs. They're too restless and may need to escape outside with more ease during the night to shift. Which is our chamber?*"

"*Second floor, third door on your left. Have you eaten?*"

"*I have.*" He opened the door, stepped inside and after he closed it, slid the bolt across. With a bundle of clothes in his hands, he walked to the trunk. Still shirtless and his upper body glistening in the firelight, he folded his clothes inside and closed the lid. "Are you warm?"

"Very." She shoved the covers back and shuffled across to make room for him.

"What did Nessa wish to speak to you about?" He toed off his boots, unstrapped his sword and propped it within easy reach against the bedside table then set his wrist daggers on the top next to a flickering candle.

"She, ah..." Goodness, every inch of his sculpted body rippled with muscle, his shoulders and arms so wide and strong. Her fingers itched to touch his chest, to glide down and stroke over every one of his contoured abs.

"Isla?"

"Huh?"

Grinning, he eased one hand onto the bed and leaned over her. "When you look at me like that, little bear"—he trailed one finger down the white cotton between her covered breasts—"I just want to devour you."

"Aye, please do. I wish to be devoured." She pressed her palm against his chest and embraced his heat. Everything within her both swelled for more and settled with that one simple touch. "True peace only comes when you're close. I'm lost otherwise."

"The same goes for me. You're my life, all that I'll ever need or desire. When you disappeared within that vortex, I experienced a moment of sheer panic I never wish to live through again." His eyes heated to a fiery golden hue. "You're my mate, the only woman I wish to share my life with. I love you, and living without you is no longer possible."

"I love you too." She'd never survive without him.

"Isla, I have something very important to ask you, and preferably before you make me lose all thought as you usually do when I slide into bed with you." He licked her lower lip, his voice whisper soft. "I need to bind us together in every possible way. I want you not just as my mate, but as my wife. Will you do me the great honor of marrying me?"

She looked deep into his eyes, her heartbeat racing at the desire burning in his own. "There's no other for me, only you, and I long to be your wife." Happiness surged and bubbled inside her. She grasped his arms and dragged him down on top of her.

"I will love no one as much as I love you." He slid her hair over her shoulder, played with the ties at her neck then slowly slid the bow free and eased one hand inside the folds of her shift and cupped her breast.

A wave of pleasure rippled thought her and she wrapped one arm around his neck and drew him closer still. His mouth, so sensuously soft was a temptation she couldn't resist and no longer intended to. "Kiss me."

"Aye, I need to kiss you." He kissed her, his tongue sweeping over hers then delving deep.

A surge of desire flooded her and an ache pulsed between her thighs.

"You smell incredible." He scented the air, a low growl rumbling from his throat. "Like vanilla and spice and something very, very nice. It's heady, an essence I've never caught the aroma of before."

Males could scent when their mate was at her most fertile as well as any change when they conceived. It had always been that way, from the very beginning.

"It calls to the very heart of me, as if you're—" He took another deep breath in, wriggled down the bed and lifted the hem of her nightgown. With both his knees between hers, he nudged her legs even wider then glided one hand along her inner thigh then over the crease of her groin. He stopped, held his position, his fingers smoothing over the flatness of her belly. Slowly, he lowered his head and with a soft sigh, nuzzled and kissed her right where he'd touched. "You're carrying my cub."

She sank her fingers into his gloriously silky hair and smiled. "That would be cubs. Nessa has seen we're to have two sons, both seers. They'll be tangled together at birth, neither older than the other as they emerge into this world. That's what she needed to speak to me about. The vortex opened because I'd conceived, the only way to be sure the two lines had merged. That set the prophecy in motion."

"I can't believe you're expecting." A sensual grin lifted his lips and lit his beautiful eyes. "Our sons will be greatly loved, by us and all of our kin. What else did she share?"

"That one day they shall lead together, their need to merge the clans their greatest desire, just as it shall be ours. She also said to allow my father to aid in their guidance, to teach them all they needed to know of their skill." She rose up on one elbow, pushed him onto his back then slung one leg over and straddled his legs. Oh, he was hard, very hard, his cock tenting his kilt. "I am becoming very quickly distracted by you."

"As I get with you." He palmed the back of her head and drew her mouth down to his. He kissed her, long and slowly, and just as she needed until she was an achy, hungry mess.

Rubbing against him, she sank her mind deeper into his. *"Never let me go."*

"Never. You are mine, throughout all time."

* * * *

Iain wanted Isla with a thirst he'd never known before. He'd longed for her from the very beginning and he'd long for her until the end of his days. Still, he should slow things down, and he would if her soft little moans weren't driving every thought from his head. Kissing her, delving into the honey recesses of her mouth had his cock pounding for release.

"Need more." She rocked against him, stirring him even further.

It was too much. He rolled her onto her back and rose over top of her. He swept his tongue inside her mouth, the need to touch all of her riding him hard. He wanted to trace every inch of her smooth skin with his hands and tongue, to show her with his devoted touch just how much he loved her. He finished undressing her, tossed her nightgown onto the floor and reveled in the sight of all her creamy flesh. Cupping the fullness of her perfect breasts, he licked then sucked her nipples deep inside his mouth, first one and then the other. He couldn't get enough of the sweet taste, and that pure womanly scent of hers swirled around his senses and drove him half insane. "I want to eat you."

"Aye, please." She loosened his belted plaid, removed it and feasted her gaze on him. "I want to take you in my mouth."

His cock lengthened and a sizzling pressure buzzed at the base of his spine. Just the thought of her wrapping her luscious pink lips around him made him so damn hard he might come with her gaze on him alone. "Later, much later." He rolled her onto her belly, slid one arm underneath her waist and lifted her onto her hands and knees. "I have a desperate need to be as one with you first."

"Oooh, I like this position." She wriggled her cute bottom, her glorious hair the shade of rich chocolate sliding off her back and brushing the pillow as she peered over her shoulder at him.

"As do I." He adored it. He crawled over top of her, the warmth of her back heating his chest and his bear rumbled its pleasure. Head dipped, he razzed his teeth over the sensitive flesh at her neck. "I need to mark you."

She stretched and offered her neck fully to him. "After you mark me, I'm going to mark you."

"And I'll demand you do." He licked her skin, sucked it deep inside his mouth and trailed one hand down her belly and over her smooth mound. He caressed her clit and when she arched back into him her breasts swayed from side to side and brushed his arm. "Stay still, love, otherwise this is all going to end far quicker than I'd like it to."

"Can't. Need more, now." She reached underneath her and palmed his balls, her soft touch nearly undoing him. Then she slid her fingers around his shaft, rubbed the head over her wet folds and coated him in her delicious scent.

"Do that again." He wanted everything, all that she offered.

"Maybe later, much later." She shoved her backside into his groin and impaled herself on his cock before he could even register what she intended to do. His breath whooshed out then she lifted up, almost coming to his head before sliding right back down on top of him again. "Bite me. Now."

He arched fully over her, razzed his teeth over her neck and rubbed her clit. What his woman wanted, he'd give her. "Ready?"

"Aye." She pushed back against him and he thrust into her until his balls slapped the inside of her thighs then he gave her exactly what she'd asked for. He growled and bit down. Her inner muscles clamped around him and squeezed him so perfectly, over and over and he came in one long hot rush, her core bathing him in liquid heat and her body clenching so tightly around him, he soared into heaven right along with her.

As he came back down, Isla went limp in his arms and he gently lowered her onto her front. She turned her head a touch, fingers moving her hair and exposing the other side of her neck. The compulsion was too strong not to take her offering and he licked the sensitive spot then imbibed on her again. "You've got a hungry little bear inside of you."

"One I'm not allowed to let roam for several months." A breathy answer. "Which means you'll need to satisfy her well and truly between the sheets to keep her happy."

"Then allow me to see what else I can do." He rolled her onto her back and with his hands either side of her pillowed head, slid his cock slowly inside her then even more slowly out. Raw pleasure still coursed through him, her body tugging at his as he pushed in again.

She sighed, so dreamily. "I don't know where you end and I

begin."

"We're one and always will be. All I want is to stay buried deep inside you and never leave the heat of your body."

"I want that too."

Blood pounding, he gave into both their needs and built her pleasure with his cock alone. He stroked in and out of her, his hunger matching hers as he offered her his very soul and she offered him the same in return.

* * * *

Lying in bed with Iain a warm weight overtop of her, Isla slowly came back down from the orgasm from heaven. She stroked his broad shoulders, skimmed down his arms and over his thick forearms. "I love making love with you. Is it later yet? I want my turn."

"Soon. Allow me to take care of you first." He slowly rose, strode to the side table and dipped a cloth in the basin of water and wrung it out. Carefully, he knelt between her legs, parted her thighs and caressed that part of her still tingling for more. She closed her eyes and moaned as the soft cotton moved over her flesh.

Iain fondled her clit, slid his fingers inside her and with his head between her thighs, flicked his tongue along her folds and sent a pulse of desire bursting through her. She gasped and widened her legs farther, her fingers sliding into his wavy black locks as she cradled his head to her. "I feel too much."

"Or maybe not enough." He thrust a second finger in as he kissed her in the most intimate way. Such exquisite pleasure radiated through her core and rippled outward then sizzled all the way to her fingers and toes. In a deep and delicious rhythm, he moved, every flick of his tongue and stroke of his fingers making her rise once again. He built her desire, higher and higher until it consumed her.

Clinging to his mind, she shared her pleasure, and before she lost all thought, she searched and skimmed the hard length of his cock and caressed his hot flesh, pumping him in time with how he stroked her.

He moaned, long and low then took her mouth in a hot kiss even as he continued to stroke his fingers into her so completely and perfectly below.

"I love you." She stroked him harder, until an orgasm beckoned and her hips lifted instinctively to his. "Inside me. Skin to skin."

"Aye, skin to skin." Hands on her hips, he slid his cock through her slick folds and drove deep into the heart of her. A deliciously decadent smile lifted his lips, his gaze hot and hungry on hers. "Open wider for me."

"Always." She spread her legs farther and he pushed higher, his mouth covering hers in a hot and passionate kiss as he did. Then he thrust hard and fast and her body tightened its hold on him, her mind anchored in his as they reached that pinnacle together. They toppled over the edge then flew, their thoughts of love barreling over each other's as they soared to the stars.

It was a long time later before her senses finally returned and his next whispered words soaked in. "Now it's later, much later."

She grinned then finally got to play with him just as she'd wished to.

Chapter 11

Isla awoke in the morning and stretched as the dawn's sunshine slithered between the wooden shutters over her narrow window and offered the promise of a beautiful day to come. She turned over and smiled as Iain lay snoozing beside her, his hair a rumpled mess and his jaw holding a razz of stubble. She buried her nose into his neck and nipped his flesh. "Wake up, sleepyhead. We've a mission ahead of us and we need to get moving."

"Is it morning already?" He rubbed his eyes with his knuckles.

"It surely is." She crawled over top of him, hopped out of bed and slid the burgundy ambry curtain to one side. The maid had hung a number of gowns and she selected the first one. With the mountainous folds of rich red fabric in hand, she eased the material over her head. The heavy layers whooshed down her body and brushed the polished floorboards. So weighty and cumbersome. She wouldn't be able to move as fast as she usually did in such clothing. She searched the floor for her jeans. Gone, and so too was the rest of her clothing. The maids must have taken it all with them when they'd cleared everything away.

"What's wrong, love?" Iain lumbered toward her, every inch of him so deliciously nude.

"I, ah, lost my clothes. I'll get them back later."

"Here, allow me to aid you in dressing."

"It's you who needs to get dressed."

With a sinful grin, he pulled the front laces of her gown together along the edge of the low-cut neckline and before tying a bow, lazily kissed the upper swell of each breast, his gaze on hers. "I haven't yet told you of the plan we devised last night."

"What was decided?"

"Firstly, to save all within the village." He scooped her gown's matching slippers from the ambry shelf and knelt at her feet. He lifted one foot and she held onto his broad shoulders as he slid the slippers on. "And secondly to ensure Finlay and Kirk find their mates. We'll head to the village along with Gilleoin, Nessa and Sorcha this morning. You missed meeting Sorcha last night. She's lovely, even reminds me of my own mother."

"That sounds like the perfect plan. I'm totally on board for a visit to the village, as well as to stand at your side when the war begins." She crossed to the looking glass and ran a brush through her hair, pinched her cheeks and rolled her shoulders, her resolve firm.

"You'll be nowhere near the village when the war begins. That I can assure you."

"I won't be parted from you, and you need a compeller on your side in this war, and don't make me compel you to agree."

"Has there ever been someone who hasn't fallen for your skillful voice?" He stepped into a pair of black leather pants and fastened them at his waist, donned a billowy-sleeved white shirt and shrugged on a tan padded cotun made of strong rawhide. The cotun would certainly protect him against the cold as well as aid in buffering any strike of a blade.

"Not a soul."

"Your compelling though, it can't halt an arrow if it were aimed at you." He tugged on his black boots, crossed to the side table and lathered soap in the basin of water. He smeared the bubbles along his jaw then picked up his dagger. Within the looking glass propped in front of him, he bent to the task of shaving.

"No, but I can halt the one who is aiming an arrow at me." She held back his shoulder-length locks from falling forward into the suds.

"That's only should the one aiming at you be able to hear your compelling command in time."

"I can halt an entire army bent on attacking if I'm given the chance. I'm going to be at your side when the war begins."

"I've seen how very strong you are and swift of mind, but you can't outrun an arrow, or a dirk tossed at you, or a raised sword." He ran his blade in a smooth line from the top of his jaw to his chin.

"I think we're about to have our first fight."

"As do I."

A rap sounded. "It's Finlay. You two up?"

"We are, just a moment." She opened the door. "Can you outrun an arrow, Finlay?"

"No, and why do you ask?" He leaned against the doorway in forest green pants and a black tunic, his Matheson plaid draped over one shoulder.

"Your brother is about to get obstinate and I don't like it."

"Morning, all." Kirk marched along the gloomy passageway wearing black battle leathers and his sword belted at his side.

"You appear ready to fight." She motioned them both in.

"I am, for the life of my mate." Kirk entered, kissed her cheek and said, "Thank you for bringing us all through to this time. I haven't said that yet and I should have."

"The same goes for me." Finlay pulled her into a hug. "I'm most grateful to be here, that you fell through a portal. Now I just need to find my mate."

"Exactly how grateful?" She smiled slyly at Iain over her shoulder. "Enough to convince your brother to include me in the battle?"

"Don't agree to a word she says. She is going to be nowhere near the village come June the eleventh." Iain shook his head then swiped his dagger from ear to chin and in the small space between his nose and lips. Done, he splashed the remaining suds away and dabbed his face dry with one of the folded cloths. He leaned his leather-clad butt on the edge of the side table as he faced his brothers. "My wife-to-be is expecting twins, two boys and both highly skilled seers."

"Well, well." With a smile, Finlay slapped Iain on the back. "We needed to hear some good news today. Congrats."

"Stupid brotherly allegiance." She snorted and closed the door with a thunk. "I'll find a way to get around you all. I know what I'm doing and I can remain safe while I do whatever I need to do."

"Your wife-to-be sounds like she means business." Kirk shook Iain's hand then frowning, set one palm over his sword hilt.

"What's up?" Iain asked him. "You look particularly worried."

"Finlay and I've been talking about our previous searches for our mates. Over these past five years, my searches have only ever led me north-east across the Highlands, in and around Loch Shin. I mentioned so to Nessa this morning. She's assured me that my mate holds a touch of fae blood and that all I need to do to find her is to follow my senses, that she may or may not be at the village. Only time will tell."

Finlay nodded at Iain. "For me, for the first time in five years, I was actually driven toward this area during the night of the last full moon. Except I only got halfway into the chase when I sensed your excitement. I knew the moment you'd found Isla that you had. I couldn't continue on and was drawn back to Ivanson Castle. My mate could be anywhere as well." He clasped Iain's forearm with one hand and Kirk's with the other. "Although deep inside, I feel strongly that my mate is close."

"A sense I haven't yet felt." Kirk grasped Finlay's forearm then took hold of Iain's forearm and closed their circle until the three of them stood together, each facing the other. "I have a feeling it'll be more difficult to find my mate. It's not like we have air travel or vehicles to get us anywhere with any speed."

"We'll find both your women all the same." Iain's determined gaze decreed his stance.

Aye, their brotherly bond was strong, their presence a formidable one, and so too would Isla stand with them, no matter what trials or tribulations reared ahead.

She crossed to the window and opened the wooden shutters. Outside, the morning sun's golden rays bathed the treetops and the green hills rising in the distance across the glistening loch. Everything looked so beautiful, not a gray cloud in the sky and certainly no threat of their enemy's attack so close at hand, although on the eleventh, blood would soak this ground and the village would burn. Something that wasn't happening, not on her watch and certainly not now she'd been given this chance to save the village that housed so many with fae blood.

She laid one palm over her belly and the precious babies she carried within. She wanted for them what she had in this moment, a future with their chosen one. This trip through time though wasn't just about Finlay and Kirk's need to find their mates, but also to ensure that the future mated bonds within their clans had the chance to flourish and grow strong. Certainly, they couldn't leave this place until everything had been set right. The time to save their clans had come.

Slowly, she turned and rested back against the stone windowsill. The 'power of three' stood before her, the most beautiful sight and she was excited to be a part of them.

Chapter 12

The morning following his daughter's disappearance, Murdock Matheson stood at his solar window on the second floor of Matheson Castle overlooking the inner courtyard. The ancient elm tree swayed in the brisk breeze coming in off the loch, its branches scraping against the thick stone walls of the keep. A seagull circled overhead then flew toward him and landed on the closest branch while below, his men trained, their swords slashing and steel clanging loud throughout the keep.

The 'power of three' had now been unveiled and although he couldn't speak to Isla, he still sensed her closeness even over the wide chasm of time. Nessa, the old seer, would watch over his daughter, of that he had no doubt. Isla had conceived and she now carried a new merged line, one that would unite the two clans. And soon, Finlay and Kirk too would begin their search for their mates. It was all as it should be, as he'd seen such a short time ago in an incredible, awe-inspiring vision.

"Chief." A knock sounded. "It's Daniel."

"Come in." He smiled as Daniel walked in and shut the door. "Take a seat."

"Is Isla safe?" In khaki pants and a black muscle t-shirt, Daniel perched on the forest-green couch underneath a wall-hanging of a stunning black and white drawing of Matheson Castle as it had stood in the twelve-hundreds. He'd drawn that image himself from a vision years ago.

He motioned toward the print. "Isla is safe. She resides within the ancient House of Clan Matheson at this very moment. She made it through the vortex, and so too did Iain and his brothers. I've also contacted Michael and Megan and informed them of exactly what's happened. They're both relieved and excited for their sons and what the coming days might bring for them. They said Finlay and Kirk need to find their mates, and now they've finally been given that chance, they couldn't be more thrilled. They've also asked me to keep them informed of any further visions I might have, and I've assured them I will."

"Good." Daniel rested his elbows on his knees and clasped his hands. "The wait has been excruciating since you first told me a portal would soon open and take her away from us."

"As it has been for me." A seer's life wasn't easy, the skill of forewarning held by so few because of the depth of control needed to wield the ability. "Last night I also saw a vision of my grandsons, twins, and both seers. One day soon I hope to guide them just as my father guided me."

"That's good news." Daniel grinned and eased back.

"Now there's nothing more we can do but await Isla's return." He strolled to his chair behind his chunky wooden desk and sat. "You're back earlier than I expected."

"Owen and Ewan Mathie didn't put up a fight when Nathan and I cornered them at Gerry's garage. Isla would've loved to have been there when we took them down. After sedating them, we delivered them directly to our contact. The Mathies can't shift until the next full moon, and I was assured they'd both be well contained on those nights."

"Perfect." He closed his eyes and focused on Isla. He couldn't force a vision, but he could remain alert if one were close to surfacing. Images fluttered behind his eyelids then shimmered into brilliant life.

Isla wore a gown of rich red and long lacy sleeves that brushed her fingertips. She watched Iain, Finlay and Kirk as they stood in a circle, each clasping each other's forearms. A soft smile lifted her lips and a twinkle lit her golden eyes, just as it used to light her mother's. Her soft words, when they came, echoed all around, so hypnotically powerful. "It's time," she said to the men before her. "Together, we're going to save the villagers, find Finlay and Kirk's chosen ones and return home to our true time."

Iain tipped his gaze toward her and she skipped across to him, slipped under his arm and stood within the circle of three. "And no one is leaving me behind."

Murdock chuckled. Iain would soon learn that no one could tame a compeller, not when Isla loved as greatly as she did. Her mate was the one man she could never survive without, and at each other's sides, they would remain at their strongest.

Aye, the 'power of three' was a formidable presence, but at their center stood his daughter. Isla would ensure their coming mission never had the chance to fail, of that he had no doubt.

Coming in Highlander's Passion, Book Two is Finlay's story.

Coming in Highlander's Seduction, Book Three is Kirk's story.

Author's Note

Clan Matheson descends from a twelfth century man called Gilleoin, a man who was believed to have been from the ancient Royal House of Lorne. The name Matheson has been attributed to the Gaelic words Mic Mhathghamhuim which means "Son of the Bear," and the clan chief's arms carry two bears as supporters. In the twelfth century, clan Matheson settled around the area of Loch Alsh, Loch Carron, and Kintail, and gave their allegiance to clan MacDonald whose chiefs were the Lords of the Isles. Clan Matheson became a large and powerful clan with a force of around two-thousand men, although by the middle of the sixteenth century they'd diminished greatly in size and influence due to the blood feuds raging across the isles at that time. This warring left them to possess less than a third of the original Matheson property on Loch Alsh.

Interestingly, the other main branch of clan Matheson lived near Loch Shin, Sutherland, at this time, and it was when I discovered this piece of vital information that the story I wished to tell of this once mighty clan and the whispers in ancient times of their ability to shift into the form of the bear became clear.

For the purposes of this story, I chose for Gilleoin to have two sons, both when they came of age forced to go their separate ways, one remaining at Loch Alsh and the other traveling farther afield to an area near Loch Shin. Those sons would then lead their own clans, yet would one day once again merge to bring the legend surrounding clan Matheson back to life. It's time for the whispers to reignite. Clan Matheson are the "Son of the Bear."

This story is woven with as much accuracy to the period and locations as possible, although any mistakes made are mine alone.

This book forms part of *The Matheson Brothers* series, and each story within it is stand-alone.

Please feel free to search for any of my other works. I simply adore strong heroines, and have a ton of fun matching them with their honorable alpha heroes.

Also available in paperback
Scottish Historical Romance

Traveling through time…for a Highlander.

Highlander Heat Series

Highlander's Castle, Book One

Highlander's Magic, Book Two

Highlander's Charm, Book Three

Highlander's Guardian, Book Four

Highlander's Faerie, Book Five

Highlander's Champion, Book Six

by Joanne Wadsworth

Looking for more sexy Scottish adventure?

Read on to catch a preview of the next book in
The Matheson Brothers series – Finlay's story.

Highlander's Passion

The Matheson Brothers, Book Two

by Joanne Wadsworth

Gilleoin – The Legend

In the twelfth century, a man named Gilleoin became the first and only known man to hold bear shifter blood, an ability gifted to him by The Most High One. His clan was called Matheson, and when he mated with a woman carrying faerie blood, they created a line shrouded in secrecy, a line that far into the future, now neared extinction...

The Seer – Nessa

The ancient House of Clan Matheson, led by Gilleoin, the Chief of Clan Matheson, Scotland, 1210.

As the midnight hour struck, Nessa, her clan's fae-blooded seer, crossed the darkened inner courtyard toward the gate, her black fur cloak secured tight over her shoulders. Torches mounted on the stone walls spread their flickering glow across the stony ground and up along the battlements where double the number of guardsmen stood on duty in battle attire, their claymores holstered at their sides.

Restless after all that had transpired this eve, she hastened her step and passed through the arched gate then traversed down the winding trail toward Loch Alsh which reflected the beauty of moon's glow on its white-capped waves.

On a fallen log, she perched and slowly bowed her head. So many thoughts consumed her mind. A seer's life was never easy and she'd been gifted with a skill she upheld to the best of her ability, although none other than a seer could have ever foreseen the terrible battle about to ensue. Their enemy, the Chief of MacKenzie, would soon strike at their very heart and blood would flow within the village nestled farther along the loch. Some of the villagers, those directly descended from the faerie prince who'd wed their chief's daughter two centuries past, held a touch of fae blood and as such also held rare and divine skills. Never would she allow her fae kind to be harmed, and thankfully earlier this eve she'd received aid in her mission, help that had miraculously come from another time and place.

Three identical warrior brothers of immense strength—Iain, Finlay, and Kirk—had traveled through a portal from the future into her time, three men who could shift shape into the form of the bear. They could draw claws and roar as Gilleoin and his two sons could. These three warriors, known as the 'power of three,' had also arrived with Iain's mate, Isla, a fae-blooded shifter from the future, the daughter of Murdock, her clan's chief and seer.

Over the years and the centuries separating them, Nessa had come to know Murdock through joint visions. They held the same beliefs and goals, although unfortunately in the future where he lived, Gilleoin's shifter clan now neared extinction and required a new infusion of fae blood within their shifter line, an infusion she needed to make certain occurred.

Eyes closed, Nessa once again searched deep within her mind. Visions couldn't be forced, but with this level of worry and anxiety rolling through her, it usually meant one was close to rising. Images teased the periphery of her mind and she grasped ahold of them.

Her granddaughter hurried through the forest nearby, her fae skill of fire flaring beyond her control, each step she took scorching the earth underfoot. Arabel raced toward an icy pool of water, fell to her knees at the edge and plunged her hands into the cool depths. Steam billowed into the air, and she slumped forward, her shoulders heaving as she gulped deep breaths.

Nessa's sight swirled again with another barrage of images, her second vision coming hard on the heels of her first. Finlay, one of the three brothers who'd arrived from the future, jogged through the postern gate on the other side of the castle then dropped to all fours, and in a sizzling display made the Change. One massive bear with silky black fur lumbered into the woods, his beast restless as he pawed the ground then rose up on his hind legs and roared. His thunderous growl stated his frustration, that he searched for his mate and he wouldn't leave this place until he'd found her.

For five long years Iain, Finlay, and Kirk had been searching for their chosen ones in the future. Iain had found Isla recently, but Finlay and Kirk's search could only now truly begin, their women residing here in this time. Both brothers were now far closer to finding their mates than ever before, and all here wished to aid them.

With care, she returned her focus to Arabel. Her granddaughter still knelt at the pool's edge in a cloud of steam, a sense of loss and frustration rolling through her.

"Why is this happening to me?" Arabel whispered into the dead of the night. "I've never lost control for no reason afore."

Nessa would need to keep a close eye on Arabel. Not all was as it seemed, and that knowledge reverberated strongly through her. Aye, as she always would, she'd watch over each and every one of her kin, including the newcomers who'd arrived from the future. None of them need ever face their difficulties alone, not when she remained close by.

The Seer – Murdock Matheson

Matheson Castle, led by Murdock Matheson, the Chief of Clan Matheson, a man with dual shifter-fae blood, Scotland, current day.

Alone in the misty moonlight, Murdock Matheson paced the battlements overlooking the night-shrouded waters of Loch Alsh. Either side of the castle, the forest stretched for miles upon miles, providing their shifter-fae skilled clan descended from Gilleoin's firstborn son's line with the perfect level of isolation they needed from the rest of the world. As the seer and chief of his clan, he kept a constant eye on his daughter, Isla, as well as the three warrior brothers known as the 'power of three' who'd traveled through time with her to the year twelve-hundred and ten.

His daughter now resided over eight-hundred years in the past, and although he couldn't speak to her, he still sensed her closeness even over the wide chasm of time. So too Iain would never allow Isla far from his side, not now they'd finally found each other and completed their mated bond.

Aye, what a mission they all now had ahead of them. Finlay and Kirk now searched for their chosen ones, a mission of untold danger as the coming battle with the MacKenzie loomed. Hell, he desperately wished he could aid his kin in saving their fae people, although glad he was for Nessa. The seer of ancient times would watch over them all, of that he had no doubt.

Gripping the thick stone crenellation, he brought Nessa's image to the forefront of his mind. Visions came as and when they pleased, but he sensed one was close. With his eyes closed, Nessa's image fully crystalized. She sat on a fallen log under a midnight moon before the very loch he too stood before, although so many centuries past. Her head was bowed and a black fur cloak covered her shoulders, a vision cloaking her mind. At times, if the same vision assailed them, they could tap into each other's thoughts and speak across time.

With focus, he drew his attention on his ability and the vision Nessa was under. A half mile from Nessa, a young woman with long blond tresses knelt at the edge of an icy pool of water, her hands submerged within the cool depths and steam puffing into the air. A fire-wielder. The steam signified her attempt to cool herself, and her frustration and loss of control pervaded the air. Something was amiss.

He returned his focus to Nessa and whispered to her across time, "Nessa, I've caught images of the fire-wielder losing control of her skill. Who is she?"

"Murdock, 'tis good to speak to you again. The fire-wielder is my granddaughter, Arabel. The lass rarely loses control of her skill, and only if her emotions swing too widely, although we've certainly experienced quite the upheaval this eve with the arrival of the newcomers."

"Is there anything more I can do to aid you?"

"If there is, I shall let you know." The care and concern in her voice shimmered through. "Murdock, Finlay's bear rides him hard. He is desperate to find his mate."

"The war approaches and he fears losing her in the coming battle, before he's even had the chance to find her. The fae village must be saved, Nessa, so that we might once again have hope. Gilleoin's future shifter line must survive."

"Aye, I will keep a watchful eye over all. 'Tis time to right the wrongs of the past, and this is our chance." Nessa touched her heart. "Until we speak again, my friend."

"Aye, take care." He touched his heart in return.

Nessa's image slowly fluttered away and he opened his eyes and released his grip on the rough stone crenellation. Farther along Loch Alsh, where the village had once stood, a sacred memorial standing stone tormented him with its solitary starkness. The loss of his fae kind within the village had been a burden that had consumed him for years, as it had Nessa. The unjust death of the villagers could be no more. Aye, the time to save their people had arrived and clan Matheson must once again rise to its greatest strength. The "Son of the Bear," couldn't be allowed to falter.

Chapter 1

Near the ancient House of Clan Matheson, Scotland, 1210, four days following.

Arabel's skin heated as the fire she held deep within her body raged again for release, now a fourth night in a row. She hurried along the forest trail near the castle with her twin sister at her side and emerged before a pool of water encircled by towering pine trees. Moonlight beamed through the thick foliage overhead and lit the loch's dark, glassy surface. "Thank you for coming with me, Julia," she breathed in a rush.

"Should you ever have need of me, I'll always be here."

"I'll need to fully submerge myself this eve. My heat flares too greatly to simply dunk my hands in." She turned around and gave her sister her back. "Be careful as you unlace my gown."

"Of course." Julia stepped in behind her and worked the laces loose. "Oh, you are so very, very hot. Why is this happening now?"

"I wish I knew, as well as why my very soul aches as if I've lost someone important."

"We might very well lose those we love if the MacKenzie isnae stopped." Julia wiped her brow as she stepped back. "Please, you must cool yourself. These flares must stop."

"If only there were others with my skill I could go to for guidance." She was the only one of her fire-wielder kind left, hers one of the rarest of their kind's skills. Swiftly, she shoved the long sleeves of her gown down then wriggled her hips. The soft layers of burgundy fabric slithered down her legs and swished to her feet. Grasping the folds of her ankle-length shift, she jumped out of the puddle of velvet and dashed across the damp, mossy ground and scrambled onto a large boulder.

The loch deep within the forest, small, private and perfectly round, beckoned with the promise of its cool depths within and its ability to bring her heat back down. With one deep breath, she leapt and down she went, the blessedly cool water closing in over her head. Bubbles fizzed around her, and in the murky dark, she kicked upward and emerged. Steam billowed all around, so thick her sister on the grassy bank became shrouded in the dense cloud that plumed. Treading water, she called out, "Are you all right, Julia?"

"I am. What of you?" Julia flapped a hand through the air as she moved around the pool to a clearer spot, her cheeks rosy and red.

"The water soothes me."

"I wonder," Julia said as she plopped onto a rock in her forest-green skirts, her brow wrinkled in concentration, "if the four elements have something to do with your loss of control. Fire is one of them."

"Mmm, fire, water, air and earth."

"Your first loss of control also occurred the night the newcomers arrived, the *air* so disrupted."

"Yet the air has settled while my fire continues to rage. What are they like?" Her sister had been to the fae village over the past few days and met the travelers as she had not.

"Iain is the eldest of the three and never allows Isla far from his side, no' since she is expecting. She holds both shifter and fae blood and in the future her clan lives here, while the others come from farther across the Highlands."

"Does she hold an ability?" Her fingers still itched with heat and she waved them through the water.

"One of the strongest, the skill to compel. With her hypnotic voice alone she can command any around her. The last man at the village to hold that ability passed away five and twenty years ago. 'Tis wonderful to know it continues on."

"What of Finlay and Kirk?"

"They're causing quite the stir as they search for their mates. The lasses are all quite giddy with excitement, hoping they might be the one. So far no matches have been made." She leaned forward. "The warriors are identical in every way and 'tis almost impossible to tell them apart."

She could well understand the excitement. The mated bond was an all-consuming one any couple would wish for. "I hope they find their women soon."

"So do—" Frowning, Julia rose and narrowed her gaze. "Something's wrong. Your aura has suddenly changed."

"For the better I hope."

"Nay, it now spikes out with sharp tendrils of cold-fire blue. I've no' seen the cold-fire enter your aura since our parents passed away."

"Are you certain there is cold-fire present?" She touched her chest, the soul deep ache within her having not abated one bit. Such feelings of loss could bring her cold-fire about.

"It bleeds deeper as I speak, which I dinnae like." Julia walked toward the trail's entrance. "I'll go to Nessa for an answer."

"You're leaving right now?"

"Aye, she willnae leave our village kin during their time of need."

"I'll come with you."

"Nay, remain. I'll sail rather than take the forest path, and I'll send a guard to keep watch over you." She lifted one hand and disappeared down the trail.

Wonderful. Now her aura was changing too. She hardly needed to burden her sister or their clan with all of her problems when a deadly battle loomed.

Kicking out deeper, she sent rippling waves swelling out. The cooler water continued to wash over her, as did the soul deep ache, an endless throb she couldn't disperse. Long minutes passed as she swam back and forth.

"Are you Arabel?" A warrior rode free of the forest path, his horse snorting misty air as he hauled it to a stop.

"I am." She slowed, treaded water. "Who are you?"

"Finlay Matheson. I passed Julia along the trail. She asked me to guard you, said your fire skill had flared." He dismounted in one easy and swift move.

"There's really no need to stay. I'm fine."

"How bad are these flares you're experiencing?" He slung his horse's reins over a low branch, knotted the leather then strode toward her, his great plaid secured over his broad chest with a silver pin and belted low at his waist with a leather girdle. Midnight-black hair curled onto his shoulders and his golden gaze met hers with unwavering intensity. He had the eyes of a shifter, just as Gilleoin and his sons, Kenneth and Ivan, did. So mesmerizing.

"Naught that the cool water cannae disperse."

"I see." His biceps flexed as he palmed the hilt of his mighty sword. "I'm intrigued by your skill."

"Julia wonders if the four elements of fire, water, air and earth are involved in the flares."

"The vortex that hauled us through did so within mere minutes. The air was thick and swirling fast." He propped one booted foot on the boulder next to her discarded gown. "I can't see any heat emanating from you."

"Mayhap I've cooled sufficiently." She swam toward him and at waist-depth, slogged through the water and joined him on the grassy bank. "Do you mind checking?"

"Not at all. Tell me what to do." He extended one hand as if wishing to take hers and she shook her head.

"Nay, you must no' touch me unless all is well." She lifted her hand and turned it palm over. "If you will, bring your palm closer to mine, but halt at the point where you feel my heat. That will give me a good indication if my fire still flares too strongly."

Slowly, he lowered his hand until it hovered a little above her own. "There's no heat that I can sense, although being a shifter, my blood runs hotter than most."

"Then touch me." Her words whispered out, and far too breathy. "I mean—"

"It's all right. I know what you mean." Grinning, he picked up one of her long golden locks and curled it around his finger. "Your hair is now dry, as is your shift, so you must be emitting some heat."

"I dry my clothing with merely a thought. I am never wet for long." She shuffled closer, drawn by the spark in his golden eyes. "Where exactly do you live in the future, Finlay?"

"I live far across the Highlands toward the east near Loch Bear. Ivan, Gilleoin's second-born son, weds Bethia and becomes chief of his own clan at Ivanson Castle. Bethia doesn't hold any fae blood, which is why Ivan's line is shifter alone as Kenneth's is not. I'm one of Ivan's direct descendants." Eyes twinkling, he caught her hand and brought her palm to his cheek.

"Mmm, you feel lovely and warm, just how you're supposed to."

"Are you flirting with me?" Surprise took her. No man ever had.

"Are you aware I'm here to find my chosen one?" He kissed her fingertips.

"All the lasses are." A flare of heat pulsed from her and she jerked back and broke their contact. "Oh, my apologies. Did I burn you?"

"Not at all." He held out his hand for hers again. "Allow me to touch you."

"'Tis best I return to the water."

"Then if you're returning, so am I. That water looks heavenly." He kicked off his boots. "I've also got a very playful bear who longs for a dip, that's if you don't mind sharing that water."

"You cannae swim with me. I'm a fire-wielder. Where there is fire, there is hot water."

"I love hot water, or cold. It matters not." He knelt at the loch's edge and swept one hand through it. "This isn't hot at all, a little warm, but not hot."

"It will be far hotter if you hop in with me." Her heat had flared when he'd touched her and she didn't doubt it would do so again if he came too close. "I truly dinnae need a guard even though my sister asked you to watch over me. Your brothers must surely need you."

"I left them behind. I felt a desperate urge to return early. They'll be here first thing in the morning so for tonight, or for however long you need me, I'm yours."

"Your mate could right now be at the castle and in remaining here with me, you might miss out on meeting her." She walked backward into the water and a tiny puff of steam rose. She was still too hot, but at least she was cooling.

"Possibly, but that's not going to deter me from guarding you. I gave Julia my word I'd remain." Sword belt unstrapped, he propped his weapon against the boulder then divested himself of his wrist daggers before unpinning his kilt.

Oh goodness. He was now clothed in naught but his white tunic that fluttered against him mid-thigh. She fanned her flushed cheeks at the sight of his strongly muscled legs. Never had a man unclothed himself while she watched on. She sank lower and kicked away. "Have any within your clan ever discovered that there is no mate when you come of age?"

"There are a good dozen unmated men who've been searching for their chosen ones and have had no luck in finding them."

"What if they never find them? Or you never find yours?"

"Should that happen then I will find the strength to move on. My parents and brothers would never allow me to wander too far from my clan. They hold me to the present and always will. You appear to be a strong swimmer."

"I am."

"Good, because my bear truly does wish to play and you're the only possible playmate in sight. Catch me if you can." He dove and disappeared beneath the night-shrouded waters.

Twirling around, she searched for his shadow within the loch. There wasn't even a ripple on the surface to mark his movement or a bubble to prove he'd released even the tiniest mouthful of air. She hadn't played in the longest time and even as dangerously alluring as he was, she couldn't help but dive after him. She kicked hard as she scoured the bottom of the loch for him. He had to be down here somewhere, and her lungs were near to bursting so his surely must be too. Ah, there. A hazy streak of white. His tunic. That had to be him. She clamped a hand around his ankle and he twisted around, his hair swirling about his face as he beamed at her. Then he wrapped his arms around her waist and kicked them both upward. They emerged in a burst of bubbles and she gulped in air. "I didnae realize you intended to swim at the bottom of the pool."

"I had to test your strength." He tightened his hold on her, kicking for them both. "You don't seem hot at all to me."

"Hold onto me any longer and I will surely burn you." She slipped out of his arms, tossed her feet in the air and went under. As she kicked across to the far side of the pool, a heated wave rippled out from her. His touch had her emotions rising and her excitement building. Never had she played with a man in this way before. 'Twas delightful, naughty even. Underwater, she swam then surfaced when she made the boulders bordering the far side. Clambering onto the closest one, she made it just in time as Finlay shot to the surface in a spray before her.

Grinning, he shook his dark head and sent drops flying. "So that's how you intend to play, is it?"

"You are very slow under the water." She shoved a wave of water at him and giggled. "Show me your bear, Finlay, since you insist he's the one who wishes to play."

"My bear's in a desperate mood to Change, so you're about to get your wish." He gripped the hem of his tunic under the water and held still. "The shirt has to go though. I detest shredding my clothing. Close your eyes if you need to."

She should, but for the life of her she couldn't.

"Last chance." Challenge glimmered in his eyes, a dare she couldn't help but meet.

"Go right ahead."

"As you wish." He hauled his wet tunic over his head and tossed it onto the hard rock beside her. The waters swirled about his waist as he edged closer. "This is one of the most beautiful places on Earth. It's so private and secluded. Just us within this little slice of paradise."

"Are you always like this with the lasses? Ready to unclothe at a moment's notice?"

"I've never made the Change in front of a woman before. You will be the first. Are you ready?"

She was transfixed, couldn't move her gaze from his heavily muscled chest where a smattering of hair, as dark as his head, trailed down between his contoured abs and disappeared under the water's murky surface. "I'm ready. Shift for me, Finlay. I truly do wish to see your bear."

He took another step closer, his golden eyes heating to a toe-curling hue. "Shifting causes quite a lightning bright display."

"I wield fire. There is naught as bright as that. Shift." The raw intimacy of the moment rolled through her and sparks flared from her fingertips. She sent her fire arcing high into the air then clenched her fists.

"You have such a powerful skill." He eyed the remnants still flickering on her fingertips then he made the Change and bright lights burst in a myriad of sparks. A very large bear with black fur glimmering in the moonlight rose up before her. On his hind legs, he roared.

"Come closer, Finlay." She held out one hand, desperate to touch his beast. "I willnae hurt you."

He slapped his paws down on the boulder either side of her then he nudged her hand with his muzzle.

"Thank you." She took a long breath in, sought the control she needed and sank her fingers into his silky pelt. She scratched between his ears then smiled as a purr rumbled from deep within his chest. The sound caused a strange heat to surge through her, not one of fire, but of something else. A form of heat she'd never experienced before. It pooled between her thighs and made Finlay sniff and prod her belly.

* * * *

Finlay's heartbeat thumped as Arabel petted him, as her fingers slid through his sleek coat and soothed the beast deep within him. Her stunning blue eyes, as warm as a summer sky, held glittering sparks of gold around the edges, and her scent, it swirled so temptingly around him, like honey and something very, very nice. He pushed back a little on his paws and halted. Her shift was wet from the water he'd sprayed as he'd shifted and up this close to her he couldn't help but note the thin ivory cloth pressed against her chest showing the roundness of her full breasts and a tease of pink nipple.

Slowly the fabric dried, likely from her heat and he whimpered. What was she doing to him? She'd invoked so many new emotions from him since he'd entered this secluded area and walked toward her. He should be at the castle as she'd said and searching for his mate, but the deep pull to remain with her had been unbreakable. For five years he'd been searching for his mate in the future, and never had he found her, not even during his search at the village these past few days.

She stroked him, her fingers moving in a delicious massage around his ears and under his chin. He stretched and rubbed against her for more. "Your bear is stunning, Finlay," she murmured in his ear.

He needed more of her touch, of hearing her sweet voice as she spoke so softly and sensuously to him. He prodded her belly again for more.

"I see you like being petted."

A throaty rumble. Her gentle petting soothed him, the first time another's touch had ever done so. He lifted his body higher and she rocked back then wound her arms around his neck to keep from toppling off. He licked her ear and she giggled.

"I cannae believe how soft your pelt is. It feels like furry silk, all smooth and warm. You also feel incredibly big and strong." She touched the tip of her nose to his and smiled, so beautifully his heart missed a beat. "There is something so very intriguing about you."

She more than intrigued him, her long golden locks tumbling to her waist in charming disarray and the moon's glow highlighting her high cheeks and luscious berry-red lips.

"Can you hear me at all, Finlay?"

Her question made him itch to return to her and he forced the Change, so swiftly she gasped. As a man once again, he looked deep into her eyes and said, "I heard every word you uttered, my sweet."

"There isnae a chance I'm *your sweet*." She stroked one finger along his lower lip, her mouth lifting in a teasing smile. "'Tis a shame you're back. I was rather enjoying my chat with your bear."

"My bear adored your touch, as do I."

"You are definitely flirting with me." She picked up his wet shirt lying next to her and passed it to him. "'Tis best you change."

He donned his shirt then planted his hands on the rock ·either side of her to keep her caged close. "I've never flirted, or shifted in front of a woman before. That is the truth."

"What are you trying to say?" She fixed his collar then lowered her hands.

"Perhaps I should show you." His touched her lower lip just as she'd touched his. "I wish to kiss you, to see if there is something more between us."

"Kissing a fire-wielder isnae permitted. I'm sorry, but I've clearly misled you somehow. You search for your mate and she cannae be me." She scrambled to her feet and jumped from boulder to boulder toward the bank.

"Why is kissing not permitted?" He bounded through the water, hoisted himself onto the boulder in front of her and blocked her way. "Take my hand. These rocks are slippery and I won't have you fall and hurt yourself."

"Kissing isnae permitted because I would lose control of my skill, and in the worst possible way." She shooed him to move.

"I don't think so." He scooped her into his arms then dipped his head and rubbed his cheek against hers. He coated her in his scent, until it clung to her skin and hers clung to him. Aye, his bear demanded this nearness and that he not let her go. He jumped onto the next boulder. "Since my search for my mate began, I've been led in so many different directions, although whenever I've arrived at the place where my mate should be, there was never anyone about, except for the night of the last full moon. For the first time, I was actually driven toward this area."

"Then you received a clear signal she was here." She grasped his shirtfront.

"Aye, and now I have the good fortune of holding you in my arms, I'm aware my mate is close, very close, that she might very well be you."

"That is impossible." She wriggled out of his arms and jumped onto the mossy bank.

"One can't argue with the mated bond, Arabel, not when it speaks to the very heart of the two who are soul bound." He stepped down beside her. "Do you feel anything toward me?"

"Nay, no' a thing." She frowned something fierce as she eyed his wet shirt. "Allow me to dry you." She smoothed her heated palms over his shoulders and along his chest then circling him, swished along his waist and legs. "That is better. I wouldnae want you to catch a chill."

"All I feel right now is a deep desire to jump back into that loch so when I hop back out, you'll dry me all over again." That need roared to life within him. No woman had ever laid her hands on him the way she just had, the way he wished for her to do again. Her heated touch had been sheer perfection, soft and tender, not harming in the least.

"You fascinate me, Arabel." Gently, he traced the delicate smattering of freckles across her nose and cheeks. "Do I fascinate you at all?"

"I—I—" Confusion crossed her face. "We need to leave."

She hurried around the pool toward their clothes, snatched her burgundy gown from the ground and wriggled the velvet over her head. He followed, dressed and fastened his sword and daggers as she fumbled to gather the burgundy ribbons at her back.

"Here, allow me." He slid her long golden locks over one shoulder and exposed the long length of her neck then picked up her gown's ribbons and laced her stays. Gently, he turned her by the shoulders to face him and stroked down her arms to her wrists where her gown's lacy sleeves dangled over the backs of her hands.

"Oh, your hair is still wet. We cannae have that." She ran her fingers through his shoulder-length hair, drying and tidying it, the delicious contact sending a wave of warmth across his scalp. "Is that better?"

"Infinitely. I love having your hands on me."

"You must cease talking like that." She swayed toward him and the golden sparks rimming her blue eyes glimmered before she jolted upright. "'Tis time to leave."

"Not without me." He collected his horse. "I'm your guard."

"I've roamed these forest paths my entire life. I assure you I dinnae need a guard." She walked toward the trail, the sensual sway of her hips making him want to drag her into his arms and hold her close, to smother her with even more of his scent. The desire roared through him, demanding and relentless, a need that wouldn't be appeased. His bear had found his mate and so had he, only it appeared now he'd need to convince her of that fact.

Within minutes they emerged from the woods and the thick stone walls of the House of Clan Matheson rose like an impenetrable fortress in the dark. A two-story gatehouse took pride of place in front while beyond the gate's arch, the four-story north tower house overlooked all. He stopped at the stables and handed his steed to the stable hand who hurried over to him then slung his traveling bag over one shoulder and guided Arabel through the gates and across the inner courtyard. So few of her clansmen would likely be awake at this late hour of the night, other than the guards, but since he didn't wish to wander through the great hall and disturb those warriors who had already sought their rest, he led her toward the side stairs. "Where is your chamber?"

"On the third floor." She climbed the stairs and walked along the gloomy corridor lit only by the odd candle in an iron wall sconce. The passageway remained bare of any other, each of the doors leading from it firmly shut, except for the last one. She walked inside the chamber that remained perfectly dark with not even the fire lit.

"Is this your room alone?" He followed her inside.

"It is. Which of the guest chambers have you been given?"

"On the night I arrived, I bedded down on a pallet in the great hall alongside the other warriors. I needed to remain close to the door in case my bear wished to roam, which he did in no time at all. He's been antsy this past week." But not anymore. His bear had settled with one gentle petting from her. The only woman who would be able to do that would be his mate. He set his bag down near the side table and faced her. "We were provided with all we'd need and since I've arrived, I've traveled light, as have my brothers and Isla."

"If you wish, I can ask one of the maids to prepare a chamber for you." She brought fire forth to one fingertip and lit a candle in the corner stand. Its glow flickered over her queen-sized bed with its red velvet canopy sweeping down onto the polished wooden floors.

"There's no need." He intended to stay right here where he could be close to her. "Would you like your fire lit and your chamber warmed?"

"I can manage to light my own fire. Fire-wielder, remember?" Grinning, she crossed to the window where a chilly breeze fluttered through and closed it. "I truly am fine now, my skill back under control. You can leave and be assured I'm well."

"I can't leave you, not right now." He stepped up to her, rested his hands on her shoulders and breathed in her delectable warm scent. A gentle peace invaded his soul. Holding her soothed him. He wouldn't forget this moment, the one in which he'd most certainly found his mate. Over her head out the window, the white-capped waves rolled into shore and across the bay, a sail shimmered in the moonlight then disappeared into the dark farther along the inland channel toward MacKenzie land. He'd also found her before the coming battle. Relief rolled through him. "This feels so good, standing here with you."

"I'm glad you and your brothers are here to aid us in saving the village." She slid one hand over his, her touch so soft, so gentle. His bear purred deep inside him and demanded a closer touch.

"Aye, and we won't leave until we have."

"The village is so exposed on the tip and we'll have so very little warning when the MacKenzie attacks. It does no' help that this is a busy waterway and intersects with Loch Carron and Loch Hourn."

"We can still guard these waterways well from this prominent location." He slipped one arm around her waist and drew her closer still, a hold she didn't pull away from. His bear settled even further.

"A location the MacKenzie too desires, one he intends to take, although I too will never allow him to harm the villagers. He took my parents' lives but he won't take another of my kin. I swear it, on my life."

"The MacKenzie killed your parents?" He frowned and searched her gaze. Such deep loss swirled within her beautiful eyes and that emotion bubbled up and rose within him as well. "Tell me how it happened."

"No' long after Julia and I came of age, Father entered into negotiations for Julia's marriage to the Chief of MacKenzie's third son. At the time we were allies, no' yet at war as we currently are. The MacKenzie requested a meeting, but 'twas just a ruse. As soon as my parents arrived at his castle, he had them tossed into the dungeon and then sent a demand to Gilleoin. My uncle was told to hand over his lands on the tip of Loch Alsh and in return the MacKenzie would release our parents. For several months demands volleyed back and forth until Gilleoin realized the MacKenzie would never listen to reason. That's when he set out for their stronghold with an elite contingency of his warriors. His intention was to sneak in under the cover of darkness, rescue my parents and then return with them. Instead Gilleoin discovered my parents had been slain at the MacKenzie's own hand, several months prior, afore the first demand had even been sent. He is a snake."

"What did Gilleoin do?" Rage simmered and he barely held it down. The MacKenzie had hurt his woman, something he'd never allow again.

"Gilleoin was furious and he attacked with great force then left a bloody trail in his wake. Now the MacKenzie is determined to have his retribution, to ensure he takes all Gilleoin holds as precious. Those of fae blood mingle strongly with Gilleoin's firstborn line and the MacKenzie fears the strength we'll gain from being aligned." Heat flared from her, flapped his hair about his shoulders and rippled the thick red bed canopy behind him. She gasped and jerked away. "I'm sorry. Did I hurt you?"

"Not at all. I can handle your small flares, likely better than anyone else can." He wrapped his arms around her, tucked her cheek against his chest and savored her closeness. Aye, his feelings for her were strong. Never had another woman ever brought such tender emotions to roaring life within him. From this moment forth, he wouldn't be leaving her side, not until she'd accepted their bond and the fact that they were mated.

"You would never be able to handle a strong flare, and I cannae lose any more of my fae kin, Finlay."

"You won't, not now my brothers and I are here." He stroked her back until she snuggled closer. "Do you feel better?"

"A little, but I shouldn't allow this kind of touch. I'm no' quite sure why I have."

"Because we are one and the same."

"We're not mated."

"Then try and pull away."

She pressed her hands to his chest as if she would, only she sighed and dropped them again. "An anomaly for sure. I've changed my mind. Could you please light my fire?"

"Of course." He released her even though he didn't wish to and crouched before the hearth. From a log set in a basket at the side, he tore strips off it then brought a flame to life striking flint with his dagger. Once the fire roared and spread its heat throughout the room, he rose and dusted his hands. "Would you like me to unlace your gown so you can ready yourself for bed?"

"If you dinnae mind." She turned her back and held her burgundy bodice to her chest.

"I'll never mind." He sank his fingers into her long golden-blond locks, the soft strands sliding like silk across his wrists and forearms. He eased her hair over her shoulder and exposed her back. "You have the most glorious hair. It glows like woven silk in the firelight."

"It does?" Over her shoulder, she frowned.

"Aye, and your eyes—" They sparkled like sapphires, a most striking hue with that glittering flare of gold at the edge. "I could drown in them."

"Mayhap I shouldnae have invited you into my chamber." She raised a brow. "Doing so has clearly given you the wrong idea."

"You didn't invite me. I entered of my own free will, and I would do so again and again." He loosened her lacings and unable to help himself with the sight of her neck on magnificent display again, he brushed a kiss against the long column, wishing he could damn well take a bite instead. They'd be time for that later, once he'd assured her of the depth of their bond and his commitment to her. "In the future, women rarely need aid in dressing themselves."

"How is that?"

"There are many new inventions, like zips. They have sharp metal teeth that slide together when pulled shut. I don't know quite how you deal with all these layers of fabric."

"As a child, I used to sneak a pair of trews from one of the lads when I wished to roam the woods with complete freedom. Sometimes I still do." With her bodice scrunched in her hands, she toed off her silk slippers then foraged for her nightgown in the trunk under the window before stepping behind a silk dressing screen hand-painted with a stunning field of heather.

"It's dangerous for you to roam the woods on your own." He paced her chamber, unease tracking through him. Brigands would lie in wait for just such a tempting morsel as his woman.

"Dinnae forget my skill, Finlay. One such as I hardly needs a guard. I hold one of deadliest of the fae battle skills. 'Tis just a shame I am a woman and no one allows me to use it." Her gown flopped over the top of the screen then she rustled about.

He itched to slip behind that screen and tell her exactly why she did need a guard, that it would be him and only him in the future. Instead he bunched his fists and remained right where he was. "Do you dress for bed often with male company in your room?"

"Never." She walked out, all her luscious curves hidden from his sight in a white nightgown, or at least she was hidden until she stepped between him and the golden glow of the fire. The flames lit the outline of her shapely legs to sheer perfection.

"You are a sight to behold." Touch was vitally important to any shifter, and more so between mates. He closed the distance between them and caught her hands. "Arabel, from the moment I met you, I've been drawn to you, and right now I couldn't leave you if I tried. These new emotions flaring to life within in me would only rise when I'm with my chosen one. I need you to believe that."

"I'm no' your chosen one." She stepped away and the distance she enforced had his bear rumbling his displeasure. "You must keep searching, Finlay, and I shall aid you on the morrow if you wish. I know all the lasses."

"My bear wants you, and only you." His claws sliced out. "He's hungry for his mate, and there is no arguing with either him or me." She was his, and of that he had no doubt. A fire-wielder. Aye, her skill would provide a greater challenge than most mated pairs had to deal with, but it was a challenge he was more than up for. They were soul-bound, a match in every way, and he wouldn't allow her skill to obstruct his path, of completing the bond and ensuring she never left his side.

Highlander's Seduction

The Matheson Brothers Series, Book Three
Kirk's Story

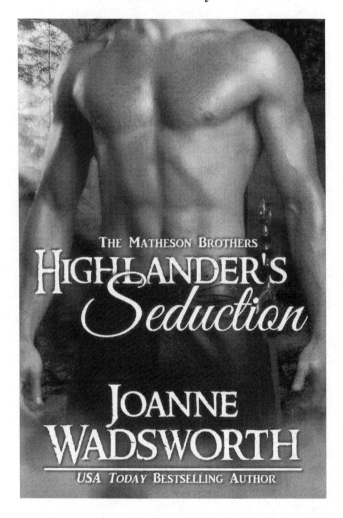

Joanne Wadsworth

I love reading romance, but even more, I love to write it. My characters hound me, demanding their stories are told. I'm happy to oblige, giving them the romance they're after, provided they can accept a little angst and adventure along the way.

In beautiful New Zealand, I live with my hubby and four energetic children, and adore using the stunning countries of the South Pacific as backdrops in many of my books. One day I hope to travel further afield, to visit the Scottish Highlands, America, and everywhere between.

Currently I have four series underway. *Highlander Heat* and *The Matheson Brothers*, are historical Highlander romances featuring strong heroines whose paths collide with their delicious Highland heroes.

Magio-Earth, is a fast-paced YA fantasy romance line, where across worlds, soul-bound mates battle against both love and land.

And in *Bodyguards*, each heart-pounding story will bring you a bodyguard and the woman he protects.

There is no greater feeling than seeing my characters come to life, so thank you for joining me...where romance meets fantasy and adventure.

To learn more about Joanne and her works, visit:
Website and Blog
http://www.joannewadsworth.com

56529906R00094

Made in the USA
Lexington, KY
27 October 2016